The Siamese Virus

A Novel by:

Glenn H. Davis Sr.

Studio of Books LLC
5900 Balcones Drive Suite 100
Austin, Texas 78731
www.studioofbooks.org
Hotline: (254) 800-1183

Ordering Information:
Special discounts are available on quantity purchases by corporations, associations, and others. For details, contact the publisher at the address above.

Printed in the United States of America.

ISBN-13:   Softcover: 978-1-964928-96-8
               Hardback: 978-1-964928-97-5
               eBook: 978-1-964928-98-2

Library of Congress Control Number: 2025912629

Table *of* Contents

CHAPTER 1

As they walked down the well-traveled hospital corridor on the way to their car, Kohora Phost tried to calm her husband, Goodwin Phost. "Honey, not so loud," she said putting her index finger to her lips as a gesture of silence. "There are other people present.

What will they think?"

"I don't give a damn," Goodwin said raising his voice. "I'm loud and I'll probably get louder." Doubling his steps to get in front of his wife, Goodwin continued his tirade.

"Why shouldn't I get loud? After being told that if I weren't a man, my symptoms indicated I might be pregnant."

"What's so terrible about that?" Kohora asked. "You know how badly I want a baby."

"That's not funny. I know how badly you want a baby, but that's your job. With me laid off too because of my hand, we still couldn't afford a baby."

"Okay, honey," Kohora said. "Calm down and wait until we get home. Then you can tell me what happened at the doctor's office."

Goodwin Phost was 32 years old, six feet one, and weighed 210 pounds. He was big all over, with well-defined muscles in the upper body. The arms were thick and of average length. His hands were large with long fingers that were perfect for his croupier job at one of the California Indian casinos. The legs were well developed, but small compared to his upper body. The face was pleasant, and he always had a ready smile for the ladies.

Kohora was a small, well-proportioned lady. At 27 years of age, she had studied to be an RN, which was her present occupation. She was five feet five and weighed 110 pounds. Her hair was auburn and of medium length. Her eyes were brown. The face was pretty, but homely. Goodwin thought she had the best-shaped legs on the planet.

They had been married for two years and didn't have any children. Kohora had wanted to start a family, but Goodwin wasn't ready until they had a little nest egg. They spent a lot of their time engaged in their favorite hobbies. Goodwin watched the reality shows and dreamed of getting on one.

Kohora worked on crossword puzzles and tended her flowers garden. After dinner, they spent quality time together, cuddling and declaring their love for each other. The drive home settled Goodwin's nerves. The house was an old thirty-year-old two-bedroom stucco house with a flat roof bordered by Spanish-style tiles. Inside to the left, there was a dining room. To the right was a medium-sized living room. A large screen TV faced the sofa. Goodwin's easy chair was to the right of the sofa. Continuing to the right were two small bedrooms. The bathroom was just outside the master bedroom. Back to the left, following the dining room, was the kitchen. There was a small island in the middle of the kitchen. Just beyond the island was a gas range with an oven below the burners. The refrigerator was to the right. A small kitchen nook where they ate their meals were completed in the kitchen.

The neighborhood was a mixture of different styles of houses, as varied as the people that lived in them. Goodwin and Kohora bought the house in May of '75.

***

As they sat in the living room, Goodwin in his recliner and Kohora sitting on the sofa to his left. Goodwin told her what had transpired at the doctor's office.

"Remember, honey, a week ago Friday, I went jogging, ran a couple of miles, and walked back to the house."

"Yes, I remember, but what does that have to do with the doctor?"

"I took a shower, relaxed for a few minutes, and then I had that big breakfast.

"The doctor kept asking me what happened to my thumb. I couldn't think of anything; except how awful I felt last Saturday morning. I was dizzy and I threw up."

"I told you what was wrong," Kohora said, "it was probably the stomach flu or you ate too much."

"Maybe, but I got over that. Whatever it was."

"Eating too much or the stomach flu?" Kohora asked.

"I don't know," Goodwin answered, "but I think I remember what I did to my thumb.

After taking that liquid protein you're always teasing me about, I twisted the wire tie that went around the wrapper that kept the bread fresh. I accidentally stuck one end of the wire into my thumb. I didn't pay much attention to it until it began to bleed. I stuck my thumb into my mouth and sucked the blood from it. It was a natural reflex for me.

Suddenly I had to sneeze, so I kept my thumb in my mouth to keep from blowing blood everywhere. I felt like a horn blower with my thumb stuck in my mouth, but I didn't spray blood all over everything."

"What did that have to do with the statement that Dr. Wells made that angered you?"

"Oh, that? He said that after I told him about nausea and dizziness."

"Dr. Wells didn't mean anything," Kohora said. "I know he didn't."

"Because you work at the hospital, he thinks he can say anything to me."

"Are you jealous?" Kohora asked.

"Of that skinny bookworm? Are you kidding?"

"Let's get back to your thumb," Kohora reminded Goodwin. "Why did you wait so long before going to the doctor?"

"I thought it would go away," Goodwin answered. "Do you think it's infected?"

"I don't know."

"You're an RN. You should know shouldn't you?"

"But I'm not a doctor," Kohora explained. "If you weren't so stubborn and macho, you would have told me about the little bump on your thumb and how it throbbed. If I hadn't insisted that you see a doctor, you wouldn't have gone today. You still haven't told me what the doctor did or said."

"He rubbed and manipulated it; asked me if I had caught it in a wringer or a vise. He was more puzzled than I. I almost forgot about the prescription he gave me."

"What prescription?"

"For the pain," Goodwin said, fumbling through his pockets. "Here it is. Would you go back to the hospital pharmacy and have it filled?"

"Yes, Dear."

***

A couple of days passed, and most of the pain ceased, but the swelling got worse. The thumb had dropped to the base of Goodwin's thumb. It had completely enveloped his thumb and was now the size of a baseball.

***

Later that night, after they had gone to bed, Goodwin sat upright and shook Kohora to awaken her. "Honey! Look at this," Goodwin said, "no pain, but look how big it is. It must be infected."

"Let me see it," Kohora said, taking Goodwin's hand in hers. She pressed the round appendage that had engulfed Goodwin's thumb. She squeezed it between her index finger and thumb. "Is it sore?"

"No, but it looks like hell to me," Goodwin answered with an exaggerated seriousness.

"I think you had better see the doctor again and let him run some tests on your thumb."

"You mean your friend Dr. Wells? What does he know? He's not much older than us. This is my thumb and my life we're talking about, and I want somebody who knows what he's doing."

"He might be young," Kohora said, "but he's up to date on the happenings in the medical field. He's always attending seminars and going to school whenever he can. He knows about genetic engineering, DNA, and all that stuff."

"I see. You've been talking to him, too," Goodwin said, frowning.

"Sure, honey, we'll talk," Kohora said. "Don't forget I work with Dr. Wells."

"I hope that's all you do with him. Don't look like that. I didn't mean it."

"Forget it," Kohora said. "Go back to sleep."

***

The next morning, "I had better get up and make that appointment for you," Kohora said, "It's almost eight thirty."

Goodwin reached out and patted Kohora on his favorite spot and said, "Thanks, honey, but before you go, I'd like for you to know how much I love and appreciate you. It's too bad, we had to spend your week off running to the hospital. This was to have been a special week for us. Our second wedding anniversary and the second year in our home."

"I had better make that appointment... Okay," Kohora said.

***

It was Thursday afternoon, around three-thirty, and Goodwin's thumb had vanished. He had covered what used to be his thumb with a wash cloth. Goodwin sat in the waiting room and anxiously awaited the nurse's call. He peeled the wash cloth back to peek at his hand. *If it weren't for you, I'd still be dealing cards. I can't work around the house. You ache like hell at times...*

"Mr. Phost," the nurse said, interrupting Goodwin's muse.

Goodwin looked up, and there was Janet Baldwin standing in the doorway with some papers in her hand. She was the wife of an entertainment booking agent who had gotten Goodwin some part-time work as an extra.

"Come with me," she said.

Goodwin got up and started for the doctor's office. When they got there, the sign said Dr. Midwiff.

"I thought my appointment was with Dr. Wells," the puzzled Goodwin said.

"Dr. Wells was busy," Janet said. "You're going to see Dr. Midwiff."

I don't want to see Dr. Wells anyway. Goodwin said to himself. "Thanks, Janet. I hope this doctor can do something for my thumb." *Janet is such a good-looking lady.* Goodwin thought. *Tall, blond... what's wrong with me? I have one of the sweetest wives.*

When Goodwin entered the office, Dr. Midwiff smiled. "What's a big, healthy-looking fellow like you doing in my office? You should be out swimming or getting a tan."

"It seems as though you've done a lot of both," Goodwin said.

"I've had my share of the sun and waves," Dr. Midwiff said.

"Look, doc," Goodwin said, extending his sore left hand, which he had covered with a small face towel. "You've got to do something about my hand."

"Calm down and let me look at it," Dr. Midwiff said, removing the towel.

Goodwin turned his head to avoid looking at his horrible appendage.

"What's wrong with your hand?" Dr.Midwiff asked, looking at the round baseball size knot that had engulfed Goodwin's thumb.

Goodwin could actually use the index finger of his left hand to play with the bubble.

"Where's your thumb?" Dr. Midwiff asked. "Your palm is a little puffy, like a small catcher's mitt…" Dr. Midwiff paused. "You could play catch with yourself. This is most unusual."

"A couple of days ago, my thumb wasn't that large," Goodwin said with his right thumb pointing toward the ceiling to indicate the previous size of his left thumb. "At first it was just the thumb, but now it looks as if whatever it is, has spread to my hand, too."

Dr. Midwiff examined Goodwin's hand very carefully. He pressed the puffiness in the palm and stroked the funny-looking bubble where Goodwin's thumb used to be. Dr. Midwiff continued probing and poking the hand, but Goodwin didn't move. "Does it ache?" Dr. Midwiff asked.

"No. Should it?"

"The way it looks, I would think there would be some soreness or pain," Dr. Midwiff said, continuing to examine Goodwin's swollen hand. "I'll have to run some blood tests."

"And after that, what's next?" Goodwin asked.

"We'll have to take it one step at a time."

"How long will this take?"

"A couple of days for the results," Dr. Midwiff replied, "but we can take the blood now. How long has it been since your last physical?"

Sweat trickled from Goodwin's forehead at the thought of blood being taken. "I don't remember," Goodwin answered, two or three years ago, I guess. I haven't been sick except for a cold or the flu, you don't get hospitalized. The last time I was in a hospital was the day I entered this world. I was circumcised and had an extra pinky on each hand was removed. After that, I haven't needed the services of a doctor."

"Since this is sort of an emergency," Dr. Midwiff said, "I'll see if they can have the test results ready by tomorrow. The nurse will show you how to get to the lab." Dr. Midwiff put the face towel back on Goodwin's round thumb.

"Thanks, doc," Goodwin said. "See you tomorrow." Goodwin gently laid his wrapped hand into the palm of his good hand. He would hold it like that until he reached the lab. *I should leave and come back tomorrow.* Goodwin told himself while he walked down the hall to the lab. *Why doesn't it ache? Why is my hand swelling? Where's my thumb?*

Goodwin's musings continued. *Do I have some kind of rare blood disease? Maybe it's an over-sized wart or a cancerous growth.* With each question, Goodwin's mental anguish became worse. He almost went past the lab when he heard a voice.

***

"Hi, I believe you are looking for me." Goodwin turned, and there was the nurse at one of the blood drawing stations. "You can sit over there," she said, pointing to a tall stool that Goodwin had almost bumped into. "Which arm shall I use to take a little blood?"

Goodwin paused, and sweat came forth from his forehead again. "This one." Goodwin said, holding his right arm up. "I can't make a fist with my left hand."

"What's wrong with your hand?" The nurse asked.

"I hurt it."

"May I see it?"

"No. Just take the blood," Goodwin replied.

"Please."

That's just like you. Goodwin scolded himself. *A pretty face will do it every time.*

"Okay," he said, removing the towel.

"It's sort of cute," the nurse said while gently squeezing the bubble that had engulfed Goodwin's thumb. "Is it sore? Does it hurt?"

"No. It doesn't hurt and it's not cute, but you are."

The nurse proceeded to draw the blood.

"How much more are you going to take?" Goodwin asked as the nurse filled the fourth vial.

"That'll be all for now," she said after removing the rubber tubing from around Goodwin's right arm and a cotton ball were placed where the needle had punctured his arm.

"I don't like hospitals. I don't like needles and I don't like…"

"That's all. You can go," the nurse said, interrupting Goodwin's mini-outburst. Kohora picked Goodwin up, and they went home.

***

Before Goodwin could get out of the car, Kohora was there trying to open the door for him. "That won't be necessary, sugar," Goodwin said. "I'm not helpless yet,"

"I don't mind. After all, you do have a slight handicap. How's your thumb?"

"What thumb? You mean where the thumb was. It's okay, so don't fuss over me."

Once they were inside, "Let me see it," Kohora said."

Sitting in his recliner, Goodwin asked, "Are you sure you want to see it?"

"Yes," Kohora said. The firmness in her voice prompted Goodwin to comply.

After looking at it, Kohora nervously asked. "What did the doctor say?" She sat on Goodwin's lap and fondled the rotund appendage just as Dr. Midwiff had done. "Did he suggest that you soak your hand in warm water or prescribe any antibiotics?"

"No," Goodwin answered, putting the towel back on his fat hand.

"What did he do?"

"The same thing you did," Goodwin answered. "He looked at it and played with it. He did order some blood tests."

"From the thumb?"

Somewhat flustered, "No. I don't have a thumb," Goodwin replied. "From my arm."

Changing the subject. "Shall I fix you a snack?" Kohora asked, attempting to get up.

"No. Stay and let me hold you a little longer," Goodwin answered.

Kohora snuggled closer. Goodwin put his right arm around her shoulder, then let it drop to her waist at the same time giving her a slight squeeze.

"Watch it, fella," Kohora said. "You're supposed to be sick."

Goodwin continued to squeeze, pinch, and fondle his wife. Caught up in the moment, he reached around with his sore hand to complete the embrace, but jerked it back in pain.

An ache that went from his sore hand up to his armpit.

"I told you to behave," Kohora said, sniggling. "Look what you've done. Did you hurt yourself? Are you in pain?"

"It was worth it," Goodwin explained. "Oh boy, I almost forgot..."

"Forgot what?" Kohora asked.

"I was supposed to make an appointment for Monday to discuss the lab results."

"I'll make it for you," Kohora said. "Meanwhile, why don't you unwrap your hand.

Let it get some air. I'd like to observe it for a longer period of time."

"Social or professional?" Goodwin asked.

"Both."

"I'm tired of this towel anyway," Goodwin said with his usual frown. "It looks out of place." Kohora watched intently. Goodwin glared at his disfigured hand.

"Is something wrong?" Kohora asked.

"No, I guess not. Maybe it's my imagination. It seemed to have grown in the last hour since I left the hospital."

Kohora reached out and took Goodwin's hand. "Where is the soreness?" She asked running her fingers in a circle up and down and all-around Goodwin's fat hand.

"Nowhere and it doesn't hurt," Goodwin answered.

"Earlier, when you squeezed me," Kohora said, "you pulled back in pain."

"I know," Goodwin said. "But it's not sore and it doesn't hurt either. Squeeze it."

Kohora complied. "See. I don't feel like it. That's what confused Dr. Midwiff."

"Where was Dr. Wells?"

"He was with another patient."

"He probably didn't want to see you after the way you acted the other day."

"I think I'll soak my hand in warm water," Goodwin said.

"Dr. Midwiff didn't tell you to soak it."

"I know what I'm doing. Nothing like an old-fashioned cure-all."

***

Goodwin went to the bathroom and filled the sink with hot water. He put his swollen hand in the water. "Ah, that felt good," Goodwin said aloud, *but wait.* He thought.

Something is missing. Mother would always put Epsom salts in the water. It reduced the swelling. Goodwin looked in the medicine cabinet. *No Epsom salts.* "Kohora," Goodwin said. "I need some Epsom salts right away."

Kohora came running. "What is it, dear?" She asked. "Did you injure your hand?"

Goodwin shook his head. "There's no Epsom salts. Will you go to the store and get some, please?"

"What are you going to do with Epsom salts? Are you constipated?"

"No," Goodwin explained. "I'm going to put some in the water while I soak my hand. It might make the swelling go down."

CHAPTER 2

The water in the sink had gotten cold. Goodwin lifted his hand from the face bowl and let the water out. *Maybe by Monday, my hand will be much smaller.* Goodwin pondered.

Since it's Thursday, I have three days before I have to report to Dr. Midwiff. Goodwin's thoughts were broken by the slurping sounds of the last few drops of water going down the drain. Goodwin's reflection continued. *I wonder why the water goes down slowly until the last few drops, then it's out with a rush. Should I wait for Kohora to come back with the Epsom salts, or go ahead and soak my hand in plain hot water again?*

"Are you still there?" Kohora asked, opening the front door and breaking Goodwin's thought pattern.

***

"Yes," Goodwin shouted back. "Bring it here."

Kohora entered the bathroom carrying a one-pound box of Epsom salts.

"Did you have to get such a big box?"

"I thought it would be better to get enough to last for a while," Kohora replied. "How much are you going to use?"

"I don't know," Goodwin answered. "Maybe a fourth of a cup per soaking."

"See, I knew I got the right size."

Goodwin turned the water on. He regulated the flow until the water felt hot enough.

Goodwin put the stopper in the sink and filled it to the desired level. Kohora put a fourth of a cup of Epsom salts in the sink. Goodwin splashed the water with his sore hand.

"Aaaah, that felt good."

"You're supposed to soak your hand and not the floor," Kohora said, reaching for a paper towel to soak up the water.

"All right, but I'm a man of action," Goodwin said. "It's hard for me to be still."

Kohora wiped up the water and left.

***

Again, Goodwin was left alone with his thoughts. *Oh thumb. Where are you? Now the damn water is cold. That's enough soaking for today. Besides, I'm getting hungry.*

He began to play with the ball that had swallowed his thumb. With his right hand, Goodwin pressed his palm, stroked the round bubble, and rubbed his whole hand like it was a new gadget he had just bought.

Goodwin let the water out of the sink and dried his hands off.

***

Holding his fat hand down and slightly behind his left buttock, Goodwin went to the kitchen where Kohora was preparing dinner.

Why are you hiding your hand from me?" Kohora asked. "Has it gotten larger?"

"No, but I'm hungry," Goodwin replied. He went to the breakfast nook, where they had their meals. Goodwin sat at the small table and waited.

If only we had children. Goodwin thought. *Kohora could stay at home and prepare these wonderful meals every day. I know she wants children, but I'm not ready.*

"Dinner is served," Kohora said, breaking into Goodwin's thought patterns.

After dinner and some lighthearted conversation, Goodwin and Kohora went to the living room to relax. Goodwin sat in his recliner. Kohora sat on the sofa. For once, his fat hand had not been mentioned.

***

"What would you like to do this weekend?" Kohora asked.

With his injured hand resting on his left thigh and his right hand on top of it, Goodwin said, "Well, I thought we would take it easy until my hand got better."

"It shouldn't stop us from taking in a movie, or will it?"

"No, I guess not," Goodwin answered, "but I'll have to keep it wrapped in a towel or something. Maybe tomorrow night."

"I could put a dressing on it."

Goodwin chuckled. "That's a good idea," he said. "Let's talk."

"What shall we talk about?" Kohora asked.

"How long has it been since I hurt my hand?"

"A week or so. I guess."

"Yes, and it doesn't seem to be getting any better," Goodwin said.

"There's not much you can do about it right now. You'll have to wait until Monday and see what Dr. Midwiff learns from the blood tests. Do you want me to rub it or put something on it?"

"Yes, that might help," Goodwin answered.

"May I see it?" Kohora asked.

"Later," Goodwin said, "I want to wash it before you put medication on it."

Without a warning, Kohora reached out and grabbed Goodwin's left arm, just above the wrist. "I told you later," he said pulling his hand away. He went to the bathroom and slammed the door behind him.

"Why are you acting like that?" Kohora shouted through the door. "Is it your hand?"

***

After a few minutes, Goodwin came out of the bathroom with his sore hand wrapped in a towel. He had a slight grin on his face. Goodwin looked at Kohora and the grin widened. He didn't have to say a word.

Now you want to apologize. She thought. "That's better," she said. "Maybe we can relax and enjoy the rest of the day."

Kohora didn't bother to comment on the towel that covered Goodwin's hand. "Sit down. Your snack will be ready in a minute or two."

In the living room, Goodwin sat down and picked up the newspaper with his good hand and fumbled through the pages as though he were looking for a particular section.

The toweled hand didn't help any. At last he found the sports page.

"Your snack is ready," Kohora said.

Goodwin made sure his injured hand was covered. He got up and went to the kitchen.

"That looks and smells good," Goodwin said. He put his arms around Kohora and gently squeezed her.

"Watch it young man. You might start something," she said.

Goodwin released his wife and sat down. He devoured the food like an eager lion cub partaking of his first fresh meat.

Kohora watched with delight. "I'm glad you enjoyed your snack," she said. "For a while, I thought you might have lost your appetite."

"It'll take more than a swollen hand to stop me from eating. Are you going to eat?"

"I had a small cup of yogurt. I hope you'll be able to caress me soon."

"The sooner the better," Goodwin said flashing a broad grin.

"I might not be as horny as you are," Kohora said, " but I do like it."

"If you wanted to make love, why didn't you say so?" Goodwin asked. "You acted as though you weren't in the mood. "I've been throwing out hints all afternoon."

"I know," Kohora said apologetically, "but every time we got too close, you seemed to be in pain. Have you become allergic to me?"

"If I am . . . ," Goodwin paused. "That's one allergy I'll die from."

Kohora looked at her watch. "It's still early. Let's watch TV before we get it on."

Goodwin looked at his wife and grinned. "You are a sleepy head and I don't want an excuse to spoil an otherwise happy afternoon"

"I'm not sleepy," Kohora said putting on her sexiest pose. "look at me. Do I look sleepy to you?"

"You never look sleepy to me," Goodwin said. "The sleep comes down all at once and you're no fun when you're sleepy."

"It has been several days and I'm hot for you," Kohora said flashing her sexiest smile.

"I'll be wide awake and ready."

"That's the way I like for you to talk," Goodwin said. "Now that we're on the same page, let's watch TV. I'll take a beer if there's one left."

"You're not helpless," Kohora said, "but I'll get the beer and you can save your energy for other things."

Goodwin checked the TV guide while Kohora went for the beer. When she returned, "There's a good movie on channel 5 at 8 o'clock," he said.

"Maybe I can freshen up before it starts. What time is it?"

"Seven-thirty," Goodwin answered, "don't be too long. I'll glance at the paper." After a few minutes, "hurry dear. It's almost time for the movie." Before Goodwin had finished, Kohora appeared in the doorway. She wore her most revealing negligee.

"Am I on time?" Kohora asked. "Will this outfit work?"

"Yes," an anxious Goodwin replied. "Let's get it on now."

"No," Kohora replied, "let's watch TV and top the night off as planned."

"Okay, I tried. If you say so, I can wait."

***

Once they were in the bed, the two lovers snuggled up to each other. After some foreplay, Goodwin was ready and Kohora was moaning in anticipation. Goodwin was about to mount Kohora, when, "Ow!" Goodwin shouted falling forward on Kohora as his swollen hand contracted.

Gasping for air, "Goodwin! You're heavy," Kohora uttered. "Raise up."

Rolling over to the side; *What in the hell is happening to me?* Goodwin thought. *My organ is limp. This can't be happening to me. I'm a young man. I wanted it so bad, too.*

"I'm sorry honey. I don't know what happened," Goodwin said.

Catching her breath, Kohora fell upon Goodwin's chest, pressing her breasts against

him. "That's okay," she said followed by a quick smooch on his lips. "There'll be other times. Go to sleep."

***

Friday: "Good morning," Kohora said when Goodwin shuffled into the kitchen. "Now who's the sleepy head? It's almost 9 o'clock. Did you sleep well?"

"What do you think?" He asked keeping his swollen hand out of Kohora's sight. "How could I sleep after letting you down?"

"I'm disappointed and I don't want to talk about it," Kohora said. "Even if I was a little forward last night. Is your hand worse?"

"No," Goodwin answered continuing to shield the fat hand from Kohora's view.

"Just more swelling."

"You mean it's bigger than yesterday?" Kohora asked.

"A little bigger," Goodwin replied.

"Let me see your hand right this minute!"

Recognizing the tone, Goodwin brought his fat hand into view and said, "It's not a pretty sight, but if you must, take a quick peep. It might turn your stomach."

"I've probably seen worse," Kohora said reaching out to examine Goodwin's swollen hand. "It doesn't look so bad. How does it feel?"

"Okay, although it's a little stiff.," Goodwin answered. *I wonder why the swelling went down?* Goodwin mulled. *But I'm glad it did.*

With his fat hand on his thigh palm up, Goodwin stroked it with his right hand.

***

An hour went by. Goodwin stroked his hand and Kohora worked her puzzle.

"Honey," Goodwin shouted. "My stomach aches and I'm hungry again . My hand looks bigger and aches, too."

"What is it dear?" the startled Kohora asked dropping her pencil. "Did I hear you say you were hungry? You ate a little over an hour ago. . . ."

"So?" Goodwin inquired. "I'm hungry now and I feel nauseous. Hurry."

"Hold on dear, I'll have lunch ready in a jiffy," Kohora said. "Keep your shirt on."

When lunch was ready, Kohora placed the large bowl of tuna salad on the table in front of Goodwin. She sat across the table from Goodwin and watched.

Goodwin let his fat hand rest on his left knee while he devoured several helpings of the large tuna salad Kohora had prepared. He paused for a break.

"You were hungry," she said. "Would you care for more?"

"No. Thanks anyway," Goodwin replied after wiping his mouth and putting the crumpled napkin on his plate. *My hand feels better. It's not aching anymore.* Goodwin reflected. *I must have really been hungry.*

Goodwin pushed away from the table and raised his fat hand from his left knee and looked at it.

"Well, I'll be. Kohora, look at this," he said holding his swollen hand up for Kohora to look at it.

"Some of the puffiness has gone down," she said. "Looks good. What did you do?"

"Nothing, but who cares as long as it has stopped aching."

"Let me feel it,"Kohora said. She reached over and took her husband's fat hand and rubbed it as though it were a pet.

"Ooo . . . that felt good," Goodwin said, " . . . in your hands."

The afternoon went by quickly and before they realized it, they had eaten, Kohora had cleaned the kitchen and it was almost bedtime again. Kohora read while Goodwin tried to solve a chess problem. When he finished it, Goodwin went to the bedroom. He looked in the mirror. *I could use a shave.* He thought. *Maybe I'll be able to make love tonight.*

"Are you ready for bed?" Kohora asked.

"Not yet," Goodwin answered. "Can you help me put my pajama top on? It's hard for me to get my sore hand through the sleeve."

Kohora went to the bedroom where she proceeded to help Goodwin put his fat hand through the sleeve in his pajama top.

"Whew. It was a tight fit, but we made it," Kohora said.

"Next time we might have to cut the sleeve," Goodwin said. "I don't like the idea of cutting my shirt sleeves."

"We'll have to wait and see," Kohora said.

"I think I need to shave," Goodwin said. "It'll only take a few minutes."

Goodwin left and went to the bathroom. While holding the tube of shaving cream under his left armpit. He removed the cap and squeezed some of the lather from the tube into his right hand. Goodwin used his index and middle fingers to spread the lather on his face. *Dammit!* Goodwin thought. *Trying to shave with one hand is hard. I can't pull my skin tight so I can get a closer shave. Maybe I should call Kohora to help me. No. I'll have to tough this one out. This left hand is useless. I feel so helpless.*

"Goodwin dear, what's taking you so long?" Kohora asked. "I have to come in. There are some last minute adjustments I would like to make."

Rushing to finish shaving and using his one good hand, Goodwin repeated the previous action. This time it was the short square bottle of his favorite after shave lotion.

After removing the top, Goodwin leaned forward tilting the half filled bottle allowing the liquid to run onto his right hand. He dabbed some of the wayward cologne on his face.

Looking at himself in the mirror; *Not bad.* He thought. Goodwin wrapped his fat hand again, "Come in," Goodwin said. I'm done."

When they squeezed past each other in the doorway, Goodwin noticed that Kohora had not rolled her hair up. "How long will you be?" he asked.

"Not too long," she answered.

***

Goodwin went straight to the bedroom. He sat down on the edge of the queen size bed. *It shouldn't take Kohora long.* Goodwin reminded himself of his wife's beauty.

Hair hanging down her shoulders the way I like it . . . no undies on. . . .

"Here I come," Kohora shouted while taking a running start and diving on top of

Goodwin. He fell backwards on the bed as though he had been hit with a right cross. The towel on his fat hand came off.

"Oh, oh, oh." Goodwin mumbled. He grabbed his left hand feigning pain.

"Did I hurt the big man? Let me soothe the pain," Kohora said while rubbing Goodwin's face, neck, chest and finally gently touching his left hand, purring with each stroke.

"You have awakened the sleeping giant." Goodwin stood up with his wife's legs wrapped around his waist. Goodwin took a couple quick steps and flipped the light switch off.

"How romantic," Kohora whispered squeezing Goodwin's neck. "it's ten-thirty-one and all is well."

Goodwin turned to face the bed with Kohora's arms and legs wrapped tightly around him. Goodwin gently placed Kohora on the bed. This was what he had waited for. Then it happened. "Ow!" Goodwin yelled as he tried to steady himself. He fought to remain conscious, but to no avail.

"Goodwin!" Kohora said rolling off to the side to avoid the fainting Goodwin, and landing on the floor. After turning the nightstand light on, her first reaction was to call 911, but Goodwin moved. He turned over on his back and looked at his wife.

"What happened?" he asked. "Is your love too strong?"

"Not unless you've become allergic to me," the puzzled Kohora replied. "Every time we try to become intimate, you have a reaction."

"That's funny," Goodwin said although he didn't crack a smile.

Kohora reached over and gave her husband a pat on his chest. "Relax," she said. We'll try to make love another time. Sleep tight."

***

Around nine a.m. that Saturday morning, Kohora hopped out of the bed. She looked at her sleeping husband. Goodwin was lying on his back. The fat hand was curled against his left thigh. His right hand was across his chest. Kohora blinked her eyelids to make sure she wasn't looking at an illusion.

"Honey. Wake up," she said.

With his eyes barely opened. "What's the problem?" the startled Goodwin asked.

"Your hand has gotten bigger. Does it ache?"

"A little," Goodwin answered.

"Look at it," Kohora said. "Look !"

The pain intensified. Without looking, Goodwin sat up and slid his legs over the side of the bed and seized his wrist and held it as if it were trying to attack him.

"Honey! Are you trying to choke your hand?" Kohora asked tugging at Goodwin's right wrist. "Let it go. It's changing color. You've cut off its circulation."

Beads of sweat popped from Goodwin's forehead. "My hand was trying to curl up on me like it was trying to flex my bicep," the flustered Goodwin said letting his wrist go.

"Look what you've done." Kohora pointed to the bruise that partially circled Goodwin's left wrist.

"Forget the hand. I'm hungry," Goodwin said looking sideways at his left wrist.

Kohora slipped her robe on and went to the kitchen. She opened the refrigerator and took out a package of cheese. Kohora broke off a piece of cheese and took it to Goodwin.

"Maybe this'll hold you until breakfast is ready," she said.

With his good hand, Goodwin snatched the cheese from Kohora. "I've never seen you like this," Kohora said. "Can you wait until the food is ready or shall I serve it as is?"

"How much longer dear?" Goodwin asked licking his lips while stuffing the cheese into his mouth and giving it a chew or two.

"Just a few more minutes," Kohora replied.

"Okay I'll wash my face and put my clothes on," Goodwin said.

After awkwardly pulling his PJ bottom off and putting his sweat pants on, Goodwin noted that it was easier to wear sweats than struggle with a zipper on his regular pants.

Now Goodwin was ready to remove his PJ top.

After pulling the sleeve as far down on his fat hand as he could, "Kohora I need your help again," Goodwin said. *This is humiliating.* Goodwin thought. *When the swelling goes down, I won't have this problem. If I do, I won't wear a shirt.*

"What's wrong dear?" The concerned Kohora asked returning to the bedroom.

"I can't get my big hand through my sleeve."

"Let's see," Kohora said gripping the end of the left sleeve. The sleeve was stuck at the fattest part of the swollen hand. She gave it a slight tug, but the hand was too large.

"Forget it!" The frustrated Goodwin said. "I'll keep my PJ top on for now. I'm still hungry. I'll be okay. After I eat, we can try again."

Kohora returned to the kitchen. Shortly afterward, "Come and get it," she called out.

***

"About time," Goodwin said. When he saw the food that Kohora had prepared, "You are truly wonderful, but that's enough for both of us."

"I'm not hungry," she said. "Enjoy."

"You expect me to eat all of that food? Ten biscuits, three big sausage patties, four eggs and a quart of orange juice?"

"Yes, you said you were hungry. That should fill you up for a while."

Goodwin ate all of the food. "That wasn't as much as I thought it was," he said. "Do we have any ice cream?"

"Yes, If I didn't know better, I'd think you were eating for two people."

"Don't be funny," Goodwin said. "Do we have any cake?"

"No, do you want me to run to the store and get some?"

"That's okay. I'll take a bowl of ice cream a big bowl."

"Get what you want," Kohora said setting the bowl and ice cream on the table in front of Goodwin. "Is that all you can do? Eat?"

"What do you mean? 'Is that all I can do?'" Goodwin angrily asked. "I'll make you eat those words soon."

"When? When?" Kohora asked. "I get horny when you talk like that."

"Same here!" Goodwin said.

After Goodwin finished the half gallon of ice cream, he went to the den and settled into his big easy chair.

"Do you want to take your PJ top off?" Kohora asked. "Or are you going to keep it on all day?"

"Might as well," Goodwin replied. "We aren't going anywhere."

With his appetite satisfied, Goodwin read the paper and watched TV, but a couple of hours later, his fat hand began to ache. He was hungry again. Goodwin got up and went to the kitchen. He opened the refrigerator. With Goodwin's recent voracious appetite,

Kohora kept plenty of deli meats, cheese and other snacks that were easy to prepare.

Meanwhile, Kohora busied herself in her flower garden. When she tired of that, she came into the house and was surprised to find Goodwin raiding the fridge.

"Why didn't you call me?" She asked. "I would've come in and fixed something for you to eat. Maybe you didn't get enough at breakfast."

Mustering a weak grin, Goodwin quickly closed the door to the refrigerator. *The last time I felt this self-conscious,* Goodwin recalled, *I was a kid.* "I was checking to see what you might fix for dinner," he finally said. "I'm not really hungry."

The hunger pangs surfaced again. Goodwin felt nauseous. He couldn't understand why his stomach would feel queasy whenever he became hungry. As always, after he had eaten, everything was back to normal. For Goodwin, an upset stomach meant that he had eaten something that didn't agree with him. This reaction to food cravings was somewhat strange.

Kohora came in and fixed the afternoon meal and they dined sufficiently. Afterward they cuddled on the sofa and watched TV. Kohora went to sleep on Goodwin's right shoulder. The fat hand dangled to Goodwin's left and rested on the sofa. Goodwin dozed off, too. Only Goodwin's throbbing hand woke him up. It was time to eat again.

I'm not going through this again. He thought. *There's something wrong with me. I can't go on like this.*

His thoughts became audible and Kohora stirred in her sleep.

"Goodwin what did you say?" Kohora asked rubbing her eyes.

"Nothing," Goodwin replied. "You must have been dreaming."

"Look," she said. "The TV has signed off. We had better go to bed."

With his manhood stiff, Goodwin asked, "What about a little bit before we retire for the night?" "Back in the day, we called it a quickie."

"Sounds good to me, but what about your allergic reaction to me? Should we risk it?"

Disappointed, Goodwin said, "Maybe tomorrow. I'll let my allergy go away, but tomorrow, we're going to get it on. Okay?"

With his fat hand, Goodwin decided to keep his PJ top on. Goodwin removed his sweats and put his PJ bottom on. They touched lips briefly and turned the lights off. The hunger pangs persisted. *I will not eat.* Goodwin reflected. *I won't let my appetite get the best of me.*

"Good night," Kohora said. "Let's do something different tomorrow."

"Like what?" Goodwin asked.

"We could go for a drive, eat out and take in a movie."

You're so sweet. Goodwin thought. *I feel so bad. I'm going to stop watching so much football.*

"What about it?" Kohora asked repeating her previous question.

"That's a good idea, but what about my hand?" he asked. "I won't be able to get it through my shirt sleeve. I can't go to dinner and to a movie topless."

"We'll work something out," Kohora said trying to ease Goodwin's frustrations.

"Let's sleep on it."

During the night, Goodwin fought the urge to eat. He did get up once and drank a tall glass of warm milk. He eased back into the bed and slept for the rest of the night.

***

Sunday morning around seven o'clock, the starved Goodwin was ready to eat. The pain in his fat hand was intense.

"Honey please get me a piece of fruit or something," Goodwin said rubbing his left arm. "My hand is killing me. Been like that all night, but I got a few winks."

Kohora jumped out of the bed. She didn't stop to put her robe on. In spite of the pain in his hand, Goodwin couldn't help but catch a glimpse of Kohora's tight little rear end.

His mind wandered for a second or two. *Wow! What I could do with that.* The left hand jerked wildly and flopped around like a newly beheaded chicken.

"Hurry dear! Bring me something to chew," Goodwin said.

The breathless Kohora returned with a six ounce cup of yogurt which she forgot to open. Goodwin snatched it from her and opened his mouth wide as he bit into the cup.

Yogurt went all over his face, but most of it went into his mouth. Goodwin squeezed and sucked on the cup until it was empty.

"Is that all?" He asked licking his lips and the surrounding area closest to his mouth.

I won't do this again. When my appetite calls, I will answer. Goodwin swore to himself.

Kohora returned in a flash. She brought an armful of snacks. Cheese, crackers and an assortment of chips. Goodwin reached for whatever was already open or he could easily open. After a minute of gorging, Goodwin fell back on the bed and closed his eyes. She had watched in awe as her husband ate himself to exhaustion. The fat hand had settled down and curled itself upon Goodwin's left thigh.

"Goodwin! Are you okay?" She asked checking one of the arteries on the side of his neck. *Pulse is strong.* She told herself. *He'll be all right. I'll clean up this mess.*

Kohora pulled Goodwin's legs around and placed them back on the bed. The fat hand seemed to be at peace. Goodwin tossed and turned, but he couldn't go to sleep.

"You might as well get up," Kohora said. "Breakfast will be ready in a few minutes.

Why don't you wash up?"

The rest broken Goodwin nodded. "Don't be too long with breakfast," he said. I feel so sleepy. I couldn't sleep because of my fat hand and the hunger cravings."

***

Kohora cleaned up the mess that Goodwin had made. She fixed a big breakfast and went to the bathroom to check on Goodwin. After cutting the sleeve on his PJ top in order to remove his fat hand, Goodwin said, "I've got an idea. We could pretend that my arm was broken and put it in a sling. My shirt would be draped over my left shoulder. That should work."

"Excellent idea," Kohora said. "I can wrap your hand in a bandage and put it in a sling and nobody would notice it."

"That sounds good," Goodwin said. "After breakfast, we'll be on our way."

"Let me shower first," Kohora said. "I won't be long."

"Meanwhile, I'll get ready," Goodwin said. "This is going to be a good day."

***

Dammit! Goodwin reflected. *I can't tie my shoe strings. I'll have to wear my sandals.*

"Are you ready?" Kohora asked. "Can I help you with anything?"

Without answering Kohora; *All I have to do is slip these sandals on and it's almost as hard as lacing my shoes.* "At last," Goodwin moaned after awkwardly pulling his sandals over his heels and on his feet.

Emerging from the bedroom, "As soon as you bandage my hand and put it in a sling,"

Goodwin said. "We'll be ready to go."

"How does that feel?" Kohora asked as she adjusted the sling that held Goodwin's bandaged hand.

"At least I won't have to let my fat hand hang down like a piece of meat."

They decided to drive to San Diego which was a couple of hours away.

***

Once there, they drove around and took in some of the beautiful country side.

"Isn't it wonderful to get away from L.A.'s smog?" Kohora asked.

"If you say so," Goodwin answered in a huff.

"What's wrong dear?"

"Nothing," Goodwin lied as the sharp pain in his left hand traveled up his arm to his head. It was migraine like. Goodwin frowned. His left hand spasmed. "It's my hand again. Maybe if I could get a quick snack until we find a restaurant, the pain might go away. It's almost noon."

"Over there!" Kohora said. "We can stop and get some chicken nuggets. That should hold you until we get to a restaurant."

Goodwin downed the nuggets as fast as he could.

"Slow down dear," Kohora cautioned, "the nuggets aren't going anywhere."

After Goodwin finished his snack, he sat back and dozed. They found a small, but exquisite restaurant and dined sufficiently. The food seemed to have taken Goodwin's mind off his hand.

"How's the hand?" Kohora asked.

"It's better," Goodwin replied. "Are you ready for the movie? The matinee is at 2pm."

***

Inside the theater, "Goodwin dear, put your left hand in my lap. I'll massage it."

"Sounds good to me," Goodwin said removing his fat hand from the sling. "Maybe I'll sneak a kiss."

During the movie Kohora removed the bandage. Goodwin turned his hand palm up so she could massage it.

"Umm, aaah, that felt good," Goodwin moaned.

"Not so loud honey. You'll disturb the other people who are watching the movie."

"Yeah, pipe down," shouted one of people behind them. "What is she doing to you?"

"Relax dear," Kohora said. "The man was right."

After the movie, they left the theater and headed for L.A. It was around 4pm.

***

At the house, Goodwin jumped out of the car and went to the bathroom. The stiffness and pain in Goodwin's hand had returned. After he relieved himself, Goodwin washed his good hand with some difficulty and dried it off. Removing the bandage from his fat hand.

Goodwin asked himself. *What's wrong with me? I can't let Kohora know how much my hand is aching. I 'll put some of this ointment on it that Dr. Midwiff gave me. Ah, feels better, but I wish the swelling would go down.*

***

Kohora parked the car in the garage and went inside. "Goodwin, are you in the bathroom?"

"Yes dear, I was about to come out."

With a tone of concern, "Is everything okay?" She asked.

"Yes," Goodwin replied. "I think I'll live until my Monday appointment. I'll fix a little snack. It's still early."

"Go ahead. I'll roll up my hair."

Goodwin took the sling off and let his fat hand hang by his side. He fixed himself a snack and went to the living room. Relaxing in his easy chair, Goodwin ate his snack.

Kohora finished rolling her hair. Later, they enjoyed watching TV. Before they knew it, a couple of hours had passed and it was bedtime. Out went the lights.

CHAPTER 3

At six o'clock Monday morning, the alarm went off. Goodwin reached over and pressed the snooze button. His appointment wasn't until nine a.m., but he hoped he could ride in with Kohora.. Having only one hand that was healthy, Goodwin wanted to have enough time to dress himself. He rolled over and tried to go back to sleep. Kohora hadn't moved. If she heard the alarm, she didn't let on. Fifteen minutes went by and Goodwin was still awake. He reached over and snuggled a little closer to Kohora. Maybe he would fall asleep now. Another ten minutes went by and Goodwin was still awake.

***

Goodwin eased out of the bed; careful not to awaken Kohora. He went to the bathroom where with great difficulty, he showered the body parts he could reach. *I should call Kohora.* He thought. *An extra pair of hands would sure work.* Because of his hand, it took Goodwin an extra thirty minutes, but that was only the beginning.

What now? Goodwin thought. *This damned hand is becoming a pain in the butt! I won't put a shirt on until I'm ready to go to the hospital for my appointment.*

Goodwin wrapped his fat hand. Put the sling on his shoulder and placed the hand in the sling. He peeked in on Kohora.

I'll surprise her and make breakfast.

***

Goodwin went to the kitchen where he prepared to make breakfast.

What the devil is happening? Goodwin asked himself. *My hand is aching again. I'll put something on it.* Goodwin stopped and went to the bathroom. He found a bottle of ointment and put some on his aching hand. *Ah, this feels better, but it still hurts. Kohora makes cooking look easy. But I'll make it.* Thirty minutes later; *I told you could do it.*

Goodwin congratulated himself. *Oh no! I'm hungry. After all, It's breakfast time. The smell of food always does this to me.*

Goodwin took a portion of a slice of bread, broke off a piece of sausage and combined it with the eggs. He opened his mouth wide and stuffed the food inside. "Mmm, that's all right," Goodwin said under his breath. *Even if I'm not a cook.*

***

Kohora awakened and followed her nose to the kitchen. "What have you done?" she asked, "don't tell me you fixed breakfast. It smells good. "I'll wash my face and hands and come back." When she returned, Kohora found Goodwin gorging himself as though he hadn't eaten in a couple of days. "You couldn't wait for me?"

He ignored Kohora's question. "Don't give me that sad look," Goodwin said. He pulled a chair out for Kohora. "Sit down my queen and enjoy."

"How's your hand dear," Kohora asked. "Let me see it."

Goodwin quickly pulled his left hand behind his back to prevent Kohora from getting a good look at it. He glanced at the clock on the wall. "I had better get a move on," he said.

If I'm going to catch a ride with you. I'll take the bus back."

"If you want to ride in with me," Kohora said. "You'd better be ready."

Goodwin went to the bedroom to finish dressing. He wrapped his sore hand with the gauze and put it in the sling. He put his shirt on draping it over his left shoulder and buttoning it as far as he could. After which, Kohora dropped Goodwin off at the hospital.

***

When they arrived, Goodwin went inside to register. There was one person ahead of him. It was seven-fifty-one a.m.

"Next," the admissions clerk said. Goodwin stepped up to the window. With a labored effort, he pulled his billfold out and removed his medical card and gave it to the clerk. Nervously, Goodwin took his fat hand out of the sling and let it drop to his side.

"I have a nine o'clock appointment with Dr.Midwiff," he said.

"What's it for?" The nurse asked while looking at her appointment sheet.

"A routine physical," Goodwin replied.

"I don't see anything here for Dr. Midwiff, but I do see your name on Dr. Wells list for nine o'clock this morning."

"Dr. Wells?" Goodwin asked. "Look again. It should be Dr. Midwiff."

Perturbed, the nurse repeated her previous statement, "It's Dr. Wells like I said. You want the appointment or you don't?"

"I don't. Let me see that list," Goodwin said reaching for the clipboard.

"Calm down, mister or I'll call security."

" Can I see Dr. Midwiff today?" Goodwin asked. "Please."

"I'll check his schedule," the nurse answered. She turned several sheets on her board.

Goodwin gently tapped the desk with impatience. Finally, "You're in luck. Dr. Midwiff has a vacancy at eight-thirty this morning."

"Whew, that sounds good to me," Goodwin said. "Thanks." *I wonder if Kohora made that appointment with Dr. Wells?*

His thoughts were interrupted by Dr. Midwiff's nurse. "Mr. Goodwin, follow me."

They stopped at the scales. "I'll have to weigh you." Goodwin stepped upon the scales. "Two-hundred-thirteen pounds. How tall are you?"

"Six foot-one," Goodwin proudly said.

"Mr. Phost, you may go down the hall," the nurse said, "there's an open door. Go in and strip to your waist. Dr. Midwiff will be there shortly."

***

In the room, Goodwin waited and waited. Finally, Dr. Midwiff entered the room.

"Hello," Goodwin said, "I wondered if you were actually coming."

"Mr. Phost," Dr. Midwiff said. "How's your hand?"

"Okay for now," Goodwin answered, "but it's stiff, aching and swelling." Goodwin unwrapped his left hand for Dr. Midwiff to see. "Look at that funny looking bubble that has covered my thumb. What is it?"

"Does it hurt?" Dr. Midwiff asked. He squeezed Goodwin's hand and worked his way up in the direction of the thumb. Dr. Midwiff gently stroked the bubble like a fortune teller would stroke her crystal ball.

"Ouch," Goodwin said. He tried to pull his hand away, but Dr. Midwiff gripped it tightly. Goodwin broke out in a cold sweat. "I feel faint." Goodwin opened his mouth as though he were going to throw up.

Dr. Midwiff quickly released the thumb. "Easy does it Mr. Phost. Can you make it to the men's room?"

"I'm okay," Goodwin said, "once you stopped squeezing what used to be my thumb."

"Explain how you felt when I pinched the globule," Dr. Midwiff said. "Be as exact as possible. Where did most of the pain originate?"

"Don't laugh, but I ached all over," Goodwin explained.

"Be more specific Mr. Phost."

Goodwin looked at Dr. Midwiff and shook his head. "Here goes. How about a headache, backache, angina, chills when you have the flu and a charley horse?"

Dr. Midwiff listened intently and smiled. When Goodwin finished, Dr. Midwiff almost fell to the floor with laughter.

"Nobody could feel that many ailments at once," he said.

"I agree doc, but that's how the one big pain felt."

"I'll have some tests run," Dr. Midwiff said after regaining his composure. "I might be able to determine what's causing your mysterious symptoms. Have you had these before?"

"No. Only the usual childhood variety," Goodwin explained. "Mumps, chicken pox and measles."

"Did you injure your thumb recently?"

"Offhand I don't remember anything at the moment."

"That's all for now," Dr. Midwiff said, "go by the nurse's station and pick up your paperwork for your lab work." Rewrapping his hand, Goodwin left for the lab to have the tests done.

***

In the men's room, Goodwin collected the urine sample and placed it in the designated cubbyhole. He returned to the lab where the EKG was taken. It had a slightly irregular pattern.

"You were probably nervous," the technician said.

Goodwin had insisted that the blood samples were last. Again Goodwin used his right arm so he could make a fist for the a smooth flow of blood for the samples. During the withdrawal of the blood, a sharp pain passed through his left shoulder down to his left arm up to his sore hand. Goodwin almost fainted. Only the x-ray was left. Goodwin went to the x-ray lab. The technician looked at the bandaged hand. "Shall I remove the dressing?" Goodwin asked.

"Yes," the technician replied. "Come over here and put your hand on this plate. Let me help you." With the wrap removed, the technician took Goodwin's hand and attempted to place it on the table.

"Relax. Don't move," she said.

"I didn't move. If I did, I wasn't aware of it," Goodwin said. He let his arm go limp.

But when the technician tried to position the hand so it would be penetrated by the x-rays at the right angle, the arm moved. Frustrated, the technician asked. "Do you want me to x-ray your hand?"

"If it means anything to you," Goodwin answered, "hell no, but Dr. Midwiff does."

"Oh," the technician said in a more subdued tone. "Can you help me?"

"I'll try," Goodwin answered. He used his right hand to stabilize his left hand. "Oo."

Goodwin moaned. "It hurts. Make it quick."

After two different positions of the hand were x-rayed, "We'll let those two positions do," the technician said wiping her sweaty brow. "Do x-rays make you nervous?"

"No. I've never had a hand x-rayed before. How long will it take to develop them?"

"Thirty minutes or so."

"I'll wait for them," Goodwin said.

"You can go by Dr. Midwiff's office and look at them."

Covering his hand with the bandage, "Will do," Goodwin said. "Have a nice day."

***

While waiting for the x-rays to be delivered, Goodwin went to the hospital's snack bar. "Hi," a familiar voice said, "how are the tests going?" It was Kohora on her break.

"I'm waiting for the x-rays to be developed," Goodwin answered. "I won't know about the other tests until tomorrow."

"What would you like for lunch?" Kohora asked.

"I'll have a couple of those sandwiches and a bowl of soup." Goodwin answered.

***

The thirty minutes went by quickly and Goodwin found himself seated in Dr. Midwiff's office. "What do the x-rays show?" Goodwin asked. He rocked back and forth in the chair. "Is anything broken? Will you have to cut my hand off?"

"Whoa! Mr. Goodwin," Dr. Midwiff said, "it's not that bad. Look." Dr. Midwiff held the x-ray up for Goodwin to see.

Goodwin stood up and went over to Dr. Midwiff's desk to get a better look. "What's that?" Goodwin asked pointing to what was once the thumb. "Where's the bone?

Dr. Midwiff shook his head. "Did you hit it with a hammer?"

"No," Goodwin replied, "I haven't done any carpentry work lately."

"Think carefully. Maybe you injured the thumb and didn't realize it."

Goodwin stared at what had been his thumb. *What have I done to it? Something did happen, but I can't put my finger on it.*

"Mr. Phost, Mr. Phost." Dr. Midwiff broke Goodwin's concentration. "Do you remember anything? I can give you some pills for the pain, but otherwise we'll have to let it get bigger before I can make a prognosis. Call me if there is a dramatic change in the size of the bubble. If the pain becomes worse, I want you here at the hospital."

"I hope that won't be necessary," Goodwin said. "I hate hospitals."

"By the way Mr. Phost, what kind of work were you engaged in?"

"I was a croupier at one of the Indian casino blackjack tables," Goodwin replied.

"With my hand like it is, I haven't been able to work."

"How long had you worked at the casino?"

"Five years before I hurt my hand." Goodwin answered, "I think I had better leave.

I've taken enough of your time. I'll probably need a snack before long."

"Shall I wrap your hand?"

"Okay, but not too tight," Goodwin replied. He left and stopped by his wife's station. She wasn't there, so he left and went home. It took Goodwin about an hour to get to his house on the bus. He hopped off the bus and walked the half block to his house as fast as he could. He was famished.

***

In the kitchen, Goodwin prepared to fix a sandwich. From the refrigerator, he took out the luncheon meat, a head of lettuce, mayonnaise and a tomato. Goodwin opened the bread box and removed the half-loaf of bread. With all of the raw materials in place, he would make the perfect sandwich. *So far so good,* Goodwin thought. He unwrapped his hand and prepared to make his sandwich. After he had spread mayo on the bread, he placed plastic wrap in the palm of his left hand. Goodwin held the lettuce against the top with the palm of his left hand and peeled a couple of leafs off. Next, he would slice the tomato. "Damn it," Goodwin said aloud as he attempted to hold the tomato and slice it.

There was a sharp pain in his left hand, followed by a knee jerk spasm that radiated throughout his arm. He wound up cutting the tomato down the middle. Goodwin's hunger pangs increased. Goodwin put the corner of the package that held the luncheon meat in his mouth.

Finally he gnawed through the plastic and ripped it open. Frustrated, Goodwin held the jar of mayonnaise under his arm against his body. He twisted the lid off with his right hand. Goodwin looked at the food and drooled; followed by stomach cramps. After he put the dressing on the bread, Goodwin was ready to enjoy his mini feast. The hunger pangs intensified. Goodwin picked up a slice of the luncheon meat and shoved it into his mouth, followed by a bite of bread, a piece of lettuce and a bite of the tomato. His mouth crammed with food, Goodwin began to chew. *This is better than I planned. I might never make another sandwich. If kohora could see me and smell my hand . . .* Goodwin went to the bathroom to wash his hand. *Maybe I should soak my fat hand again.*

Goodwin ran some hot water in the wash basin and dumped some epsom salts in it.

What a feeling. Goodwin thought. He squeezed the bubble. It wasn't sore. The whole hand seemed to have moved to brush against the fingers on Goodwin's right hand. "And thank you too," Goodwin said to the bubble, "for not aching." *What am I doing? Talking to my hand? What's causing my hand to swell and ache? Maybe I was stung by some poisonous insect when I went under the house.*

The front door opened and Goodwin's mind returned to the present. It was Kohora.

***

Goodwin rushed to the kitchen. He had meant to clean up his mess before Kohora returned home from work. With his left hand dangling by his side, Goodwin put his right arm around Kohora and gave her a big hug.

When Goodwin released her, Kohora took a deep breath and exhaled. "How's your hand?" She asked.

"It's okay. What used to be my thumb looks awful and I tried to fix a sandwich"

"Did you?"

"No."

"Let me see your hand," Kohora said. She reached for the hand.

Without hesitation, Goodwin thrust the hand forward for Kohora to look at it.

"It's not that bad," Kohora said poking it and pinching it gently. "Did that hurt?"

"No."

"Did you soak your hand?"

"Yes, and it felt good. It was probably my imagination, but the hand reacted as though it appreciated the soaking."

"Tell me about the sandwich."

"Nothing to tell. I ate it without putting it together."

"That was crude," Kohora said laughing at her husband. "You must have been hungry. Why don't you lie down while I fix dinner?"

"The dinner bit sounds good," Goodwin said, "but I'm not sleepy. I think I'll sit and watch TV. I can't continue to eat like this. Every time I eat, my fat hand gets bigger."

"Just your imagination," Kohora said walking over to Goodwin. "Your hand isn't any bigger, but the bubble that used to be your thumb is definitely bigger."

"What am I going to do?" Goodwin asked, "I can't walk around with my left hand wrapped up in a sling. It's useless."

"Relax dear. Dinner will be ready in a few. Tomorrow you can see the doctor again."

"I'm tired of that damn hospital, my hand and eating so often . . . ."

"Don't let it get you down," Kohora said. "Watch TV while I fix dinner."

"I'm worried about my hand," Goodwin said. "I feel like, like I could cut it off."

"You don't mean that," Kohora said. "You're probably hungry."

***

Thirty minutes later, "Come and get it," Kohora called out. "Dinner is served."

Goodwin was at the table in an instant. Gorging himself again.

"Slow down dear. The food isn't going anywhere," Kohora said. "That's why you're eating so often. Chew your food slowly. Digestion begins in the mouth."

"Slow is a no-no. When I go slow, I feel like I missed something."

"That could also explain your nausea," Kohora said.

Between chomps, Goodwin said, "It allows me to eat more in a shorter time."

"More food means a larger grocery bill, but if you're hungry, you'll have to eat."

After dinner, Kohora and Goodwin sat around and chatted. They even cuddled a little.

"Are you going to follow up on our cuddly-pooh?" Kohora asked. "It's about that time bedtime that is. Did you get enough to eat?"

"Can I take a rain check?" Goodwin asked. "I don't want to aggravate my hormones, and yes I had enough to eat. I hope it'll last all night."

***

It was Sunday morning between seven and seven-thirty, Kohora was in the kitchen preparing breakfast. She went to the bedroom and looked in on Goodwin. *Should I wake him up?* She smiled. *He knows how to use all of the bed when I'm not in it with him.* The left arm was extended with the hand hanging off the side of the bed. *Now's my chance to get a good look at Goodwin's injured hand.* Kohora reminded herself. She watched the bubble pulsate to the rhythm of Goodwin's breathing. Kohora continued to watch the hand. The twitching became stronger. Goodwin woke up and grabbed his left wrist. The shaking stopped.

"That's the first time I've seen a man wrestle with himself," Kohora said.

"I wasn't wrestling with myself," Goodwin quickly said releasing his hand. "If you must know, I had a bad dream. A snake had wrapped its body around me and was about to crush me. I grabbed the boa around his head and that's where you came in." Goodwin released his wrist and grinned. "You don't believe me do you?"

"Why shouldn't I believe you?"

"I don't know, but the way you looked at me . . . ."

"Let me take a look at it," Kohora said. Moving to the side of the bed where the hand was.

Goodwin shook his head, which was followed by a flinch.

Kohora grabbed the hand. "No you don't," she said putting a vise like grip on the hand. Kohora carefully inspected the bubble.

"You're worse than the doctor," Goodwin said resisting his wife with a slight tug.

Kohora continued her probing of Goodwin's arm. "What's this?" Kohora asked pointing at the large vein that ran from the inside of Goodwin's elbow down to the bubble that covered his thumb.

Goodwin looked. He examined the prominent vein. "I hadn't noticed that before,"

Goodwin answered running his index finger over the overblown blood vessel. "It's not sore even when you pressed your fingers into it. What do you think caused it to puff up like that?"

Kohora shook her head. "Maybe it wants you to give some more blood," she said. "All jokes aside, but you will see Dr. Midwiff in the morning?"

"I hoped I wouldn't have to," Goodwin said closing his eyes and dropping his head.

Goodwin raised his head up and looked at Kohora. "Should I?"

"You have an appointment and you're going to keep it," Kohora insisted.

"Okay, okay if you want me to. Is breakfast ready?" Goodwin asked.

"You eat enough for two people. If I didn't know better, I'd say you were pregnant."

"Who did it?" Goodwin asked. "I haven't slept with anyone but you."

"Don't look at me," Kohora said with a smile. "When I knock you up, you'll know it."

"How did we get off on that subject?" Goodwin asked. "You really want a baby.

Don't you? What's that I smell?" Goodwin sniffed the air.

"Oh my! That's your breakfast," Kohora answered rushing to the kitchen. She turned the burner off.

***

"Is everything all right?" Goodwin asked. as the pungency of the burned sausage floated through the bedroom.

"I'm sorry dear," Kohora said. "Don't fret honey. There's more." She dumped the burned meat into the garbage pail and wiped the burnt residue from the skillet.

"Can I help?"

"No," Kohora answered. She took the remainder of the sausage from the refrigerator.

She made three slices from the sausage roll and placed them in the frying pan.

With a disappointed look, "Is there something I can munch until breakfast is ready?"

Goodwin asked. "I'm so hungry."

"Can you wait? It'll only take a few minutes."

"No. I want something now!" Goodwin answered clutching his sore hand.

"You don't have to yell," Kohora said returning with a cup of yogurt. "Will this do?"

Goodwin reached out and took the yogurt with his right hand. He peeled the top off and threw his head back. Goodwin put the cup to his mouth and squeezed. There was a squish and a slurp and Goodwin emptied the cup of its milky substance.

Kohora laughed pointing at some of the yogurt that ran down Goodwin's chin. She returned to the kitchen and finished making breakfast, which was composed of the three sausage patties, four scrambled eggs, four slices of toast and coffee. "It's ready," she said.

***

Goodwin was there in a flash. He picked up his fork and began to eat. After a few mouthfuls, Goodwin left the table and went to the bathroom. Kohora followed closely behind him. Goodwin bent over the commode and spat the food out.

Puzzled, "Is there something wrong with the food?" Kohora asked.

"No," Goodwin answered. "I felt like I had to puke."

"Are you going to finish your breakfast?"

"Yes. I'm all right now," Goodwin answered. He went back to the kitchen and ate the rest of his breakfast, took his supplements and retired to the living room.

***

The living room was small, with a little imitation fireplace. There was a gas burning log; a six-foot sofa, a lounging chair and a gold leaf stained glass topped cocktail table.

Goodwin sat at one end of the sofa and nodded.

After Kohora washed the dishes, she returned to the living room. "Have you soaked your hand lately?" she asked gently shaking Goodwin's shoulder.

"What did you say?" The startled Goodwin asked. He withdrew his left hand as though he were trying to protect it from harm.

"Have you S-O-A-K-E-D! Your hand lately?" Kohora repeated.

"You didn't have to shout," Goodwin said. "I can hear."

"Well, have you?" Kohora asked from her hippie stance.

"No, but I'm going to right now if it'll shut you up."

"What time is your appointment for tomorrow?"

"I don't remember. I thought about missing it," Goodwin answered with an impish grin. "It's marked on the calendar."

"You're going," Kohora said, "if I have to miss work and take you myself."

Goodwin shook his head and went to the bathroom to soak his hand. Kohora stuck her head through the doorway.

"Your appointment is at ten o'clock tomorrow morning," she said.

The rest of the day went by as usual. Goodwin eating every two or three hours. He and Kohora playing with each other. The left hand aching off and on. Bedtime brought a fairly nice day to an end. They dared not to try and make love. Goodwin continued to eat around the clock.

CHAPTER 4

Monday morning after breakfast as they stood in front of the kitchen sink, Kohora was washing dishes and Goodwin stood behind her, flirting. "I'm really glad you're going to see Dr. Midwiff this morning," Kohora said. "He can discuss the test results with you. Maybe they'll tell him what's wrong with your hand. Kohora dried her hands off.

She turned and faced her husband. "Let me look at your hand. Gotcha, didn't I?"

Goodwin shook his head and laughed placing his hand in Kohora's. "I knew what you meant. I'm not a dirty old man."

Kohora took Goodwin's left hand in hers. She gently massaged it. Goodwin grimaced.

"I had better sit down," he said. Goodwin's expression didn't change. Kohora helped her husband to the living room, where he sat down in his large easy chair.

***

"You don't look well," Kohora said. "Can I get you something?"

"No," Goodwin answered and leaned back further in his big soft easy chair.

Kohora glanced at her watch. "It's almost seven thirty," she said. "Time for me to go. I don't want to be late for work. Could you give me a smile? I hate to see you like this.

Don't be late for your appointment. You know how slow the buses are."

"I'm okay. If the pain doesn't stop, I'll get a cab and go in early."

Kohora pecked Goodwin on his cheek and left.

***

The pain in Goodwin's left hand increased. The spasms continued from his hand up to his armpit. Goodwin grabbed his left wrist in an effort to control the involuntary muscle contractions. A voice inside Goodwin's head seemed to say, "call the doctor! Call the doctor!"

"I won't! I refuse to call the doctor," Goodwin said. *What am I doing? Talking to myself? I don't want to give anymore blood for tests.* Goodwin clutched his left wrist.

The bubble had begun to swell up and down to the cadence of his heartbeat. It was like someone had attempted to blow a bubble, but ran out of breath between puffs. For a moment, Goodwin forgot about the pain. When Goodwin regained his composure, the aching had stopped. He had almost called the hospital for an emergency walk in.

Goodwin held the sore hand up to get a better look at the bubble. He examined his left hand at the base where the wrist and the heel of the hand met. The vein that he used to check his pulse, was much larger. Goodwin pressed his thumb into it. There was a strong throb and a weak throb.

Do I have a slight heart murmur? Goodwin asked himself. *Dr. Midwiff didn't say anything about it. Is that what Midwiff is keeping from me? I think I'll go in early.*

It's only eight o'clock, but I need to talk to Midwiff. Maybe he has a cancellation.

Goodwin found the number for the appointment desk.

"May I speak to Dr. Midwiff?" Goodwin asked. "My name is Goodwin Phost. I have an appointment with Dr. Midwiff at ten this morning. I'd like to come in early. Has he had a cancellation?"

"Dr. Midwiff is very busy," the receptionist said.

"Lady. Would you please check?" Goodwin asked.

"Your tone of voice doesn't scare me," she said pressing the button that connected to Dr. Midwiff's office.

"Dr. Midwiff," the voice on the other end of the line said.

"What's up?" The doctor asked.

"Your ten o'clock patient wants to come in early," she replied.

"I'm very busy. Who is it?"

"Goodwin. I think that's what he said."

Without hesitation, "tell Mr. Phost I'll see him as soon as he gets here."

"What about your other patients?"

"Reschedule them," Dr. Midwiff said. "This is a special patient."

"Yes doctor," she said resuming her conversation with the restless Goodwin. "Dr. Midwiff will see you when you get here."

"Thanks," Goodwin said. He hung the phone up and immediately began to dress. He called a cab.

***

Back at the hospital, Dr. Midwiff ran into Kohora in the hall. "Kohora, could I see you for a minute?" Dr. Mdwiff asked.

"Hi Dr. Midwiff. What can I do for you?"

"Goodwin called a few minutes ago. The receptionist said he sounded urgent and wanted to come in early."

"Did he say what was wrong?" Kohora asked.

"No, but it's probably about his hand. He should be here in another forty minutes or so. Meanwhile, I'll have his chart pulled and the test results brought to my office. It's a strange case . . . a strange case. I'll call you if there are any new developments."

When Dr. Midwiff got to his office, Goodwin's chart and test results were on his desk.

Dr. Midwiff read the test results, and everything was normal. He looked at the EKG print out. *I wonder what this unusual little extra spike on top of the big one is?* Dr. Midwiff pondered. *I'll make a note of it so I can come back to it later.* Looking over the X-rays of the left hand; *Nothing unusual here except the rudimentary formation of a sea horse like skeleton that was inside the bubble that encased Goodwin's thumb. I'm unsure what this is. I've never seen anything like it before. I'll call Dr. Wells. Goodwin might remember what happened to his thumb? Maybe...*

***

"Hello, Dr. Midwiff," a serious-looking Goodwin said. "Am I on time?"

"Have a seat. What seems to be the problem?" Dr. Midwiff asked. "I don't have a lot of time, but your case is quite different. Everything was normal, except the X-rays."

"I'm not sick," Goodwin said, "but there was pain in my left arm, and I became sick to my stomach." Goodwin stared at the X-rays that Dr. Midwiff held up for him to see. "Is something broken?"

"No," Dr. Midwiff answered. "It's not that simple."

Goodwin unwrapped his hand and stroked the sac that covered his thumb. Goodwin listened intently. Dr. Midwiff showed him the bony structure encased in the sac.

"What does it mean?" The worried Goodwin asked.

"It's too early to tell," Dr. Midwiff said, "let me look at your hand.

"You going to make it better by looking at it?" Goodwin asked hesitantly.

"My, how it has grown since I saw it last," Dr. Midwiff said, taking Goodwin's fat hand in his and running his fingers over and around the sac. "Did you reinjure it?"

"If I did, I wasn't aware of it," Goodwin answered.

"Umm," Dr. Midwiff mumbled, gently squeezing the sac. "Strange indeed, strange, very strange. Would you care for a snack?"

"Yes," Goodwin quickly answered, "you must have read my mind."

"What would you like?"

A sharp tingle Goodwin jumped. A little voice prompted Goodwin.

"Did I pinch the sac too hard?" Dr. Midwiff asked. "Look at it. The sac is pulsating."

The tingle increased. "A turkey club sandwich," Goodwin interrupted. "I'll pay for it."

"It's okay," Dr. Midwiff said, "it's on me." He found himself pressing the sac to its rhythm. Dr. Midwiff stopped pressing the sac, but its cadence didn't stop. "Have you noticed the sac's action?"

"When it hurts, I'm not sure if I have," Goodwin answered. "Sometimes the pain goes up to my armpit."

"And then?" Dr. Midwiff asked.

"Nothing," Goodwin answered. "You're the doctor you tell me."

"You can help too," Dr. Midwiff said. "By telling me everything that has happened to your thumb from the beginning to the present."

"There wasn't any beginning. It just happened."

Knock, knock. "Come in," Dr. Midwiff said. "Set it over here." The boy from the cafeteria put the tray on Dr. Midwiff's desk. "How much do I owe?"

"Eight-fifty," he replied.

Dr. Midwiff pulled out his wallet and gave the young man a ten-dollar bill. "Buy yourself a soda," he said.

After Dr. Midwiff and Goodwin had eaten, "I'm all ears," Dr. Midwiff said. "You may begin. Take your time. Don't leave anything out. No matter how small it might seem."

Goodwin closed his eyes. What had he done to his thumb? When did it happen? A week ago? Two weeks ago? Nothing that made any sense came to Goodwin's mind.

"I'll leave you with your thoughts," Dr. Midwiff said, "while I check on some of my other patients. If you're alone, maybe you can concentrate better. I'll come back in about twenty or thirty minutes." Dr. Midwiff left his office.

***

Goodwin held his left hand out in front of his face nose high. Goodwin wiggled what used to be his thumb. The sac that surrounded the area, rocked back and forth. It looked like an egg with the outer shell removed. Goodwin brought the sac close to his left ear and shook it. He strained to hear something, but he didn't. A dizzy spell swept over Goodwin. He returned his hand to the desk. What had caused his dizziness?

"Any answers yet?" Dr. Midwiff asked Goodwin when he returned to his office.

"No answers, but I can tell you what has been happening to me lately."

"Like what?" The curious Dr. Midwiff asked. "Tell me." Dr. Midwiff gestured with his hands as though he wanted Goodwin to come across his desk.

"This might seem comical, but here goes," Goodwin said, "not only do I eat more, but quite often." Goodwin paused.

"Is your appetite better than before you injured your hand?"

"Yes, it is, but here's the catch. Every couple of hours, I have this craving …"

Wide eyed, Dr. Midwiff leaned halfway across his desk. "Go on, please," he said. "I don't see a clear-cut problem yet."

"If I don't eat, my left hand begins to shake. After I eat, everything is back to normal."

"Maybe we are getting somewhere," Dr. Midwiff said while taking notes. "Relax and tell me more."

"It's like I have some kind of worm in me…," Goodwin said. "Eating my food before it gets to me. That's why I'm hungry all the time, but there's more…"

"Please continue," Dr. Midwiff said, dropping his pencil and pad.

"This is confidential; right?" Goodwin asked leaning forward in the chair.

Dr. Midwiff nodded. "Of course."

Sweat rolled off Goodwin's forehead. He continued. "The other night, I wanted to make love to my wife…" Goodwin paused again.

"Don't stop," Dr. Midwiff said, "this could be enlightening."

Goodwin continued, "Like I said, I wanted to make love to my wife, but the hand wouldn't let me."

"I shouldn't laugh," Dr. Midwiff said, "but are you impotent?"

"Hell no!" The adamant Goodwin replied. "Like I said, the hand wouldn't let me."

"I'm puzzled," Dr. Midwiff said, "be more specific."

"When I was hard and ready, the hand attacked me like this," Goodwin said, curling his left hand toward his throat.

"Please forgive me Mr. Phost," Dr. Midwiff said, slipping to the edge of his chair and putting his hand to his mouth to muffle his laughter. "Goodwin. Don't leave. I shouldn't have been so how should I put it unprofessional?"

"If you're going to take this like a joke, I might as well not be here. How do you think I felt? I need help. I couldn't sleep all night. I can't make love. I can hardly dress myself. What am I going to do? You've got to find out what's wrong with my thumb and fix it."

"Now, now," Dr. Midwiff said, giving Goodwin a reassuring pat on his shoulder.

"We'll find out what's ailing you and find a cure for it. I would like to run one more test."

"Another test? More blood?"

"No blood this time," Dr. Midwiff answered. "I would like to make a small incision in the bubble...On second thought, the nurse can use a syringe and withdraw some fluid from your swollen thumb. Make some slides and look at them under the microscope. That might tell us something."

Tap, tap at the door to Dr. Midwiff's office. "Come in," Dr. Midwiff said, and in walked Kohora, wearing her two-piece white pant uniform.

"How is the sick?" She asked.

Goodwin sat upright in his chair. "If you're going to be my nurse," he said. "I might spend the rest of my life here. I feel better already."

"Shall I leave?" Dr. Midwiff asked.

"No," Kohora answered, "Goodwin will behave himself. Did he remember how he hurt his thumb?"

"No, he didn't," Dr. Midwiff answered with a tone of disappointment before Goodwin could answer. "I'm going to perform one more test."

"Don't let me stop you," Kohora said, "I was checking to see if there was anything new. Kohora pecked Goodwin on the cheek. "See you later Dr. Midwiff."

"Let's get started," Dr. Midwiff said, "I can have the results before you leave." Dr. Midwiff ushered Goodwin ahead of him.

"How long will it take for the test?" Goodwin asked. "I feel a hunger coming on."

"That won't be a problem. There's a snack bar just before we get to the lab."

***

After the snack, Dr. Midwiff and Goodwin continued on to the lab. When they arrived at the lab, Goodwin looked at the sign over the door, which read, "Laboratory". Inside, there were all kinds of syringes, scalpels, bottles, and microscopes.

"Have a seat Goodwin," Dr. Midwiff said, "I'll get one of the techs to come over and prep you for the test."

When the technician came over, she motioned for Goodwin to go to one of the little booths and sit down. "Mr. Phost, please relax," she said, swabbing Goodwin's bubble with a cotton ball that had been sterilized. She had a grip on Goodwin's left hand as she prepared to withdraw the fluid from the bubble. Goodwin nervously watched.

"Hold it right there," she said, "it'll be over before you know it." Before she could insert the syringe into Goodwin's thumb, whack; the needle, vials, and anything else that was associated with the procedure was swept to the floor.

"I'm so sorry," Goodwin said, sweat popping from his brow. "I don't know what came over me."

Two burly male nurses came out of nowhere. One of them held Goodwin, and the other one held Goodwin's left hand down while the nurse withdrew the fluid from Goodwin's bulb-encapsulated thumb. Goodwin passed out.

***

It was Tuesday morning around six am, when Goodwin finally woke up. He was still in the hospital. Kohora stood by with a reassuring smile on her face. Goodwin tried to sit up in bed.

"What the hell?" Goodwin said, struggling against the three-inch-wide canvas straps that held him down. "Am I a prisoner in some loony house? Get this crap off me."

"Easy, dear," Kohora said, "it's for your well-being." She placed her hand gently on Goodwin's chest. "Dr. Midwiff will be in and have the straps removed if you behave yourself. You became quite unruly yesterday when they tried to draw some fluid from your bubble. Afterward, you passed out. Do you remember?"

"Maybe. The nurse was trying to stick the bubble with a knife. What's wrong with my left hand? Why is it stuck out to the side? Are they going to cut it off?"

"No," Kohora replied. "Don't be so dramatic."

"What's that stuff in those bottles that's being taken from me? I thought blood was red. Is that why my thumb was swollen?"

"Nothing is being taken from you," Kohora said. "That's not blood, it's nourishment."

"Like liquid food?"

"Something like that," Kohora answered. "It's an IV."

"I need something to eat/chew," the bewildered Goodwin said, staring at the ceiling and wondering what was next.

***

Meanwhile, in Dr. Midwiff's office, he and his fellow doctors looked at the X-rays of Goodwin's left hand. "The bone at the tip of Mr. Phost's thumb has been absorbed," Dr. Midwiff said, "I wonder if there's a rare form of bone cancer we're dealing with."

"What about the sac that has covered the thumb?" One of Dr. Midwiff's colleagues asked. "What's in it? Can you burst it? Cut it off?"

"Whoa, slow down," Dr. Midwiff said, "before we do anything, we have to figure out exactly what we are up against."

"Have you gotten the report on the fluid that was removed from the bubble?" One of the colleagues asked. "That might answer some questions."

"Take a closer look at the X-ray," Dr. Wells said, pointing to the skeleton that had replaced the thumb. "What does it remind you of?"

Dr. Midwiff held the X-ray between both hands as though he were trying to stretch it.

"Like a moving tear drop," he said, "or a seahorse wobbling up and down in a fish tank."

"What do you make of it?" Dr. Wells asked. He took the X-ray from Dr. Midwiff and moved it up and down and from side to side, trying to let the light fall on the best spot that would cause the faint image of the teardrop to be seen at its best. "Well . . . what do you think?"

Dr. Midwiff shook his head. "Cut it off or let it grow larger?"

"We definitely can't cut it off," Dr. Wells said, " look what happened when we took a small sample of fluid from the sac. Goodwin went into shock."

"That's the point," Dr. Midwiff said, "we should operate while whatever it is still small. Once it grows larger, it will be more of a problem and twice as dangerous.

You saw its reaction to the needle."

***

Back in Goodwin's room, the nurse came in and removed the straps that held him to the bed. "Haaa," Goodwin sighed. "What a relief."

"Is there anything else I can do?" The nurse asked.

"No, but I hope it's feeding time around here." Goodwin wanted to sit up. *Dang it,* he thought. *I'll be glad when this mess is over.* He struggled to sit upright. The left hand was useless. Goodwin couldn't balance himself.

***

"How's the sick?" Kohora asked as she entered Goodwin's room.

"I'd like to sit up," Goodwin answered.

"Don't look so depressed, dear. Everything will be all right," Kohora said, placing her hand underneath Goodwin's head. "Relax, Darling, if you want to sit up, I'll help you."

"Don't strain yourself," Goodwin cautioned.

"I'm not going to lift you," Kohora said, "I'll use the crank. How high do you want to go?" After a few turns of the crank, "will this do?"

Goodwin nodded. *This really pisses me off. Being so helpless.*

Kohora looked away as she ruffled a pillow and placed it behind her husband's head.

She wasn't about to show any sign of pity. She pecked Goodwin lightly on his lips. Not too quickly, but a lingering side-swiping motion, similar to the Eskimo nose rubbing, but in one direction only. When Kohora was about to leave, "Not so fast, honey," Goodwin said, pulling his wife's head closer to his. He guided her lips back in line with his.

"You know what I like," Kohora said. "Yummy. That was nice." She embraced her husband as best she could. Kohora felt herself slipping as the bed moved.

"Owww!" Goodwin said, releasing Kohora.

"Did I hurt your hand?"

"No. You didn't come close to my hand. The pain came from the left side of my chest, down to my thumb."

"Maybe I'm too much woman for you... Or you might be allergic to me."

"If I am, it's one allergy that's going to kill me."

"Let's try again," Kohora said, "we'll see." She leaned over and smacked Goodwin on his puckered lips.

Goodwin's heart raced faster. "That was a wonderful feeling," he said, grimacing with delight. The tingling in his chest traveled down to his thumb again and turned to pain.

"Did I do something to hurt you?" Kohora asked when Goodwin pushed her away.

"You're too much for me," Goodwin said, clutching his left hand. "You win for now, but when I'm better, we'll see."

Both of them tried to laugh it off, but underneath the laughter, they knew something was wrong.

With a naughty grin, "Shall we try again?" Kohora asked. "I'll take it easy next time."

"Those were coincidences," Goodwin said with a renewed air of confidence. "I might give you another chance."

***

Tap, tap. "May we come in?" Asked the voice on the other side of the door.

"He's decent," Kohora said. "Come in."

The door slowly opened. "How's our most energetic patient getting along?" Drs. Wells and Midwiff asked at the same time.

"I'm alive," Goodwin answered. "No thanks to you two. Where's the food?"

"You shouldn't be hungry after all of those IV bottles you emptied last night," Dr. Wells said. "You emptied an IV bottle every hour. You were also in great pain. It was supposed to go in drip-by-drip, but the way you were consuming that stuff, the tube in your arm might as well have been a straw. We watched the level in the IV bottle change and your pain increased. Several times, Kohora checked the tube for a leak. She checked the rate of flow, too."

"Was it right?" Goodwin asked.

"That's the strange part," Dr. Wells answered, "the rate of flow was correct, but something made it run faster."

Puzzled by what he heard, Goodwin asked, "What did the X-rays show?"

"Nothing that we haven't seen before," Dr. Wells replied.

"May I see them?" Goodwin asked.

"They would only bore you," Dr. Wells said.

"I won't ask you again," Goodwin said. "Let me see the X-rays."

"Okay, okay," Dr. Wells said, shoving the X-rays at Goodwin.

Goodwin looked at them and shook his head.

Dr. Wells smiled and reached for the X-rays. "What did I tell you? Now what?"

Ignoring Dr. Wells' remarks, Goodwin returned the X-rays to him.
Taking the X-rays, Dr. Wells continued, "I checked with the lab and the results of the tests on the fluid that was taken from your thumb will be sent to us."

Goodwin and Kohora anxiously stared at each other. "Dear, there's something else you should know."

"What?" Goodwin asked. *As if I really want to know.*

CHAPTER 5

Kohora took a deep breath. "The usual mixture that we give our patients for nutrition, didn't work for you. We had to give you a special liquid protein solution in the IV before the pain and spasms stopped. We thought you had gone into insulin shock."

"Are you saying I might have diabetes?" Goodwin asked. "It might run in the family, but I think it ran away from me."

"You're clean," Dr. Midwiff said, "you don't have a trace of the disease."

Goodwin beamed. "That's the kind of talk I like to hear. Maybe I can get out of this place." In a rush, he started to get up from bed. The IV stand tottered.

Dr. Wells, Dr. Midwiff, and Kohora moved toward Goodwin at once.

"Easy dear," Kohora said, placing one hand on Goodwin's chest and the other hand behind his head.

"Goodwin, you can't leave," Dr. Wells said. He grabbed goodwin's legs in an attempt to put them back in the bed.

"Get your hands off me," Goodwin said scowling. "I'm leaving this place now!"

"Everybody, calm down," Dr. Midwiff said, steadying the IV stand. "Maybe you'd be better off at home where your wife can look after you."

"You're damn right," Goodwin said shaking with frustration. "If Kohora hadn't been here, this room would look like a storm had come through here."

"It's not unusual for a patient to behave this way," Dr. Wells said, straining to hide his anger. "Everything we've done has been for your benefit."

"When can I have some real food?" Goodwin asked, "And when can I go home?"

"Regretfully, you'll have to spend one more night here," Dr. Midwiff said. "You will be hooked up, as you would put it. Just for tonight; observation only."

They're pissing me off. Goodwin thought. *This is my last night in this place.*

"Now, Darling," Kohora said. "It's just for tonight. Had you not passed out last night, we'd be home now. Right, Dr. Wells?"

Dr. Wells nodded. "We didn't want any complications.

"What complications?" Goodwin asked. "Am I being told everything, like the truth?"

"Of course, Mr. Phost," Dr. Midwiff answered, "but we want to make sure you won't have to return to the ER. We take great pride in our profession."

Goodwin's disposition softened with Kohora's help. She bent over and caressed the back of Goodwin's neck where it joined the upper back. Her fingers shifted with the finesse of an experienced masseuse, moving back and forth between the two points.

Finally, Kohora nipped Goodwin's neck with her lips, from cheek to ear lobe and back.

"Tell me I'm dreaming," Goodwin moaned, "but don't wake me up."

"If you remain as pleasant as you are now," Dr. Wells said, "you can go home soon."

"How soon?" Goodwin asked.

"Twenty-four hours if there aren't any more tantrums," Dr. Midwiff answered. "And I'll make sure of that. You have my word."

There was a knock on the door, and in walked Nurse Spintz. "I have some food for our hungry patient," she said, disconnecting the empty bottle of formula for Goodwin and replacing it with a full one.

"Food at last," Goodwin said without paying much attention to what was really going on. "Where's the food? Was that supposed to be funny?"

"No," nurse Aida Spintz said, smiling. "This is food." She pointed to the full bottle.

Aida Spintz was from New York. She was around fifty-three years old. Short and stocky with an even mixture of closely cropped black and gray hair. She had a large nose and small thin lips that gave her the appearance of a buzzard peeking over a windowsill.

"I would like to make the bed I mean, I want to put clean linen on the bed. If you two lovebirds could break away long enough for a person to do their work," Aida said in her husky New York accented voice. "This isn't the only bed I have to change."

Kohora looked at her watch and then at Aida. "How time flies," Kohora said, pecking Goodwin on his forehead. "I had better get back to my station. Dear, can I help you in anyway?"

"No. I can help myself," Goodwin answered with a look that could have melted ice.

"Excuse me," Kohora coldly said, tripping over the wastebasket.

Goodwin saw the hurt in Kohora's eyes. He looked at her as if to say, "What'd I do?"

Before Goodwin had completely removed himself from the bed, Nurse Aida gave the bottom sheet, a short, vicious tug that almost sent Goodwin sprawling to the floor. "You men think you're so superior," she said. "You'll do anything to maintain that image."

"Woman, watch what you're doing," Goodwin said. "I could have been hurt."

With his staunchest that's a no-no look. "Be careful, nurse," Dr. Midwiff said. "You have caused the patient to hurt himself."

"Just lost control for a moment," Aida said, "it won't happen again."

"I hope not," Dr. Wells added with an air of detachment.

With both of his feet on the floor, Goodwin stood up and faced the nurse who was on the other side of the bed. "If my doctors don't mind, I think I'll take a walk." Goodwin said, gathering the IV stand and its hoses. "I need a break."

"A walk," Dr. Wells said. "Will probably calm your nerves. Don't go too far."

Nurse Aida finished changing the linen on the bed and left. There's a light tap-tap-tap on the door.

"Come in," Dr. Midwiff said.

In walked Nicia Ling, the lab technician, with a look of excitement on her face. Nicia was four feet and nine inches tall. Her long black hair was braided and worn in a bun on the back of her head. Nicia's total weight, including every button, zipper, and hairpin, was eighty pounds.

"Yes, Nicia," Dr. Wells said with anticipation, "You have the test results?"

With a slight apologetic bow, Nicia smiled and said, "I have the results, but..."

"But what?" Dr. Midwiff asked, reaching for the report that Nicia held in her hands.

"Who did the sample come from?" Nicia asked. "I forgot. Was it from a woman?"

Nicia moved her head forward as if she didn't want to miss a word of the answer.

"It came from Mr. Phost's thumb or what was his thumb," Dr. Midwiff replied as he pointed at Goodwin. "Is there a problem?"

Nicia looked at Goodwin, and then she looked at the report. She did this several times.

"What is it?" An agitated Goodwin asked. "Do I have the plague or something?"

"Excuse me," Nicia said, moving closer to Dr. Wells. In a low tone, (hoping Goodwin wouldn't hear her), "If you hadn't told me, I would have insisted that the sample came from a pregnant woman."

Dr. Wells and Dr. Midwiff looked at each other with skepticism. Goodwin stared at the doctors.

"What the hell did you say?" Goodwin asked. "That sample didn't come from me."

"There must be an explanation," Dr. Midwiff said, looking at Goodwin. "Mr. Phost, maybe you should take that walk while we get to the bottom of this."

"I'm not going anywhere," an adamant Goodwin said, thrusting his fat hand forward.

"Here, take some more fluid."

"We won't discuss it here," Dr. Wells said. "Let's go to my office."

***

Back at Dr. Wells' office, he sat at his desk. Dr. Midwiff pulled up a chair to the right of Dr. Wells and took a seat. Nicia was standing facing both of them.

"Please tell us what you found." Dr. Midwiff said, "Can you be more precise?"

With anxiety in her voice, Nicia began, "The cell structure was the same as amniotic fluid." She paused. "There was a slight variation. Maybe because it came from a man."

"Are you positive?" Dr. Wells asked. "Could there have been a mix-up?"

"There wasn't any mix-up," she said with a look of sadness spreading over her face. "I had someone else run the test twice, and I ran it two more times myself." Confidence returned to Nicia's face. During the conversation, Nicia held onto the report.

"You may go," Dr. Wells said, scratching his head. "Don't forget to leave the report."

Nicia gave the report to Dr. Wells and left.

***

The two doctors looked at each other and shook their heads. "Maybe we should send the next sample out," Dr. Wells said.

"Not on your life," Dr. Midwiff said. "We have one of the finest labs in the country.

Our staff is among the best. Let me see Goodwin's X-rays again. There was something peculiar about them."

"There were two sets of them," Dr. Wells said, "Which set do you want to see?"

"Both of them," Dr. Midwiff replied. "I would like to compare them."

"What are you looking for?" Dr. Wells asked handing the X-rays to Dr. Midwiff.

After carefully studying the x-rays, Dr. Midwiff exclaimed, "See that ammonite (a coiled chambered fossil shell) shaped object sitting atop what used to be a bone inside

Goodwin's thumb?"

"What is it?" Dr. Wells asked, "Or what do you think it is?"

"I don't know," Dr. Midwiff answered. "We'll have to wait and see."

"What are we going to tell Goodwin?" Dr. Wells asked. "He'll want some answers."

"We'll tell him that he has an infection that we haven't been able to identify," Dr. Midwiff answered. "We don't want to alarm him."

"What if it gets worse?" Dr. Wells asked. "I don't like it. What if we have to operate?"

"Let's break the good news (no news) to Goodwin," Dr. Midwiff said.

***

Goodwin was having a ball. Walking up and down the corridors, stopping every few feet to wave at the ladies. His left hand dangled by his side. *This isn't so bad.* Goodwin realized. *As long as I'm not cooped up in that little pigeonhole of a room.*

He was not aware that his IV bottle was empty, but he was getting hungry. A nurse passed him with a tray of food. He couldn't see what it was, but Goodwin hadn't eaten a real meal in the past twenty-four hours. The faint odor of the food and the nurse's swaying hips lead Goodwin astray. He hoped the nurse was going to his room. Goodwin wasn't aware that he was in the wrong wing of the hospital.

Suddenly, his left hand began to ache and tremble. *Oh shit!* Goodwin thought. *My damned IV is empty again. I had better get back to my room.*

At the end of the hall, *I must be in the wrong end of the hall.* Goodwin thought. *How did this happen?* He smiled and remembered. *Those swaying hips.* Turning around, *don't panic.* He told himself as he retraced his steps. Goodwin paused for a moment and familiarized himself with his surroundings. *I should have turned left at the corner where the information desk is.*

Goodwin's hunger pangs became more intense, and the throbbing in his left hand grew worse. Goodwin's eyesight was blurry, and he felt faint. *If I take shorter steps, I can save my energy and get back to my room before I blackout.* Goodwin's mumbling was just loud enough for a passerby to hear.

"What did you say?" She asked. "Are you okay?"

"Nothing," Goodwin replied. "I was breathing heavily."

***

Dr. Wells and Dr. Midwiff had taken different wings in search of Goodwin. It was Dr. Midwiff who found Goodwin, was about twenty feet from his room. Goodwin leaned against the wall with his left shoulder and used his IV stand to help maintain his balance.

"We've been everywhere looking for you," Dr. Midwiff said, reaching out to give Goodwin a hand. After helping Goodwin back to his room, Dr. Midwiff had a nurse bring a full bottle to replace the empty one.

"I'll have Dr. Wells paged so he'll know you're okay."

Goodwin frowned. "Do you have to page Wells? I don't like him."

"Why?" Dr. Midwiff asked. "Because he's so young?"

"Maybe."

"If you feel that way, I'll page Dr. Wells when I get back to my office. Try to get some rest. I'll see you in the morning."

Goodwin didn't want to tell Dr. Midwiff the real reason. He suspected that Wells liked Kohora, who had repeatedly assured Goodwin that their relationship was strictly professional. Goodwin believed and trusted his wife, but he didn't trust Dr. Wells.

That guy flirts more than I do. Goodwin reflected. *I guess that's why I don't like him.*

Thirty minutes had barely passed after Goodwin had returned to his room. The IV bottle was almost empty. Goodwin had tried to relax, but he felt so helpless, restrained by the feeding tubes connected to his arm. The twitching in the left hand had stopped, but the hunger pangs persisted.

If I could sneak a mouthful of food, Goodwin thought. *I'd settle for a chance to chew it, even if I can't swallow it.* Goodwin poured himself a glass of water from the pitcher that was on his small nightstand. *This is good. Almost like bouillon, and I don't like bouillon. I could have my wife smuggle me some food, but I'd have to call her and the phone might be tapped. Am I becoming nervous or what?*

***

Dr. Wells heard the page and went to Dr. Midwiff's office. "How's the patient?" He asked in a concerned tone. His face contorted with alarm. "Where did you find him? Was it wise to leave him alone?"

"Slow down, Wells," Dr. Midwiff said. "One question at a time. He was a few feet from his room. I had his empty IV bottle replaced. Goodwin was fine when I left him. I don't think he'll try anything foolish unless he gets hungry."

"That's what bothers me," Dr. Wells said. "He hasn't had anything to eat since the day he checked in. And we know how he acts when he gets hungry. When do you think Goodwin will be able to eat again?"

"He's your patient," Dr. Midwiff answered, "but he has hinted no, he came right out and said it. He wants me to take over."

"That's not why I brought you in," Dr. Wells said, "not to replace me, but help me.

I've never seen anything like that. It's a strange case. Pain originating in his left thumb, running up his arm to his chest. No fever. Allergic to X-rays. The amniotic fluid taken from his thumb. What does it all mean?"

"I don't know," Dr. Midwiff answered. "You're the expert. It doesn't seem to be cancerous unless it's a new, rapidly eating kind. That we don't know about. I thought trying that new drug or whatever it is . . . interferon."

"Do you think we'll have to go that far? We don't know what we're up against."

"Why wait?" Dr. Midwiff asked. "The sooner we begin treatments, the better our chances are of stopping whatever it is in its tracks."

***

Back in Goodwin's room, the nurse had replaced Goodwin's empty IV bottle. "It wouldn't hurt if I could have some real food," Goodwin said, giving the nurse a dirty look.

"My strength would come back."

"Don't be so grouchy," the nurse said. "When Dr. Midwiff or Dr. Wells okays it, I'll bring it to you. Until then, be satisfied that you're getting something." She smiled at Goodwin. "You'll be eating by tomorrow for sure."

"Tomorrow?!" Goodwin declared, straining to keep his anger down. *She's only doing her job.* He told himself. "I won't be here tomorrow."

Smugly, "If you don't leave now or tonight, you'll be here." She said and left.

***

There was a knock on Goodwin's door, followed by, "May we come in?" Dr. Wells asked, slightly pushing the door open and peeking inside. Dr. Midwiff was with him.

"You're already in," Goodwin said with a look of anticipated freedom. "I hope you've come to tell me I can go home. Can I pack my things?"

"Sorry. That's not why we're here," Dr. Wells said. "We would like to discuss the possibility of a minor operation."

Goodwin's expectations dropped like air from a punctured balloon. "What's wrong with me?" He asked, rattling his IV stand. "Do I have cancer?"

"No," Dr. Midwiff abruptly answered. "There's no evidence of cancer."

"What's this talk about a minor operation?" Goodwin asked. "On what?"

"We would make a small incision in your injured thumb and remove some of the tissue and run more tests," Dr. Wells said, gesturing with his hands in an effort to reassure Goodwin that the procedure was almost painless.

"When would this minor operation be performed?" Goodwin asked, mocking Dr.

Wells' previous hand movements. "If it isn't done today, forget it. I won't be around. I'm going home this afternoon or in the morning."

Bluntly, "It will be sometime tomorrow," Dr. Wells said. "You aren't leaving today."

"We would like to keep you overnight," Dr. Midwiff interrupted, "and make sure you will be able to function away from the hospital."

"Have you forgotten that my wife is an RN? I would be under the best of care."

"But the hospital is the best place for you," Dr. Midwiff said. "In case you have one of your attacks. We don't want to lose one of our most intriguing patients. We want you to feel at home."

"At home? Tell me you're kidding," Goodwin said. "Tied to this, to this rolling stand; not enough to eat; poked, prodded, and x-rayed until I feel as though I'm being prepared for some kind of...."

"You don't have to say anymore," Dr. Wells interrupted. "We're leaving. Relax if you can. Hopefully, tomorrow will be your last day. If you have any more problems, ring for the nurse. She'll have one of us paged."

During the conversation, Goodwin kept his left hand out of sight. Dr. Midwiff noticed the attempted deception. "May I see your hand before we leave?" He asked.

Without a pause or change of expression, "How does it look?" Goodwin asked thrusting his right hand forward. "Do you think I'll live?"

"On the other hand, Mr. Phost," Dr. Midwiff said, smiling and pointing to the partially hidden left hand.

"How clumsy of me," Goodwin said with an air of apology. Smiling back at Dr. Midwiff and slowly revealing his injured left hand.

Dr. Midwiff reached out and gently took it in his hand and looked it over. "It looks a lot bigger than it looked this morning. Did you bang it against something while you were walking? Is there any pain?"

"No, I didn't bang it against anything, and it doesn't hurt," Goodwin answered. "It always looks larger whenever I get up the nerve to look at it. Any bigger, I won't be able to hide it. Are you sure I can't go home tonight?"

"Just one more night," Dr. Midwiff said. "Please behave yourself."

"Do I get some real food tonight?"

"The IV will have to do for now," Dr. Midwiff said. "We'll see you in the morning if not sooner. Save your energy. You'll need it when you leave the hospital."

***

Every hour on the hour, Goodwin's empty IV bottle had to be replaced. Between those interruptions, Goodwin tried to read one of the magazines the nurse had brought.

He was restless and bored.

When am I going to get out of this place? He asked himself. *If it were left up to me, I'd leave now. Maybe I will. I'm not sick. I feel okay.* Goodwin flexed his right bicep. *I'm strong.* Goodwin nudged the bed rail with his injured hand. *It doesn't hurt. Why shouldn't I leave? There's no law that says I can't leave. But, what would Kohora say? I'll tell her I have been released. I'll call a cab and surprise Kohora.*

***

Knock, knock, and the door opened before Goodwin could get back in the bed. "What are you doing out of bed?" Kohora asked. "You're supposed to take it easy."

"What are you doing here?"

"I wanted to surprise you," Kohora answered, helping Goodwin get back in bed.

"This is a surprise. What time is it? Visiting hours are at eight o'clock."

"I'm early. You didn't answer my question. Why aren't you in bed?"

"I was going to the can," an annoyed Goodwin lied. "Is that off limits, or do I need a nurse to hold my ..."

"You'd like that. Wouldn't you?" Kohora teased.

Goodwin wanted to say yes, but he knew better. *When a man's wife questions him about the services of another woman,* Goodwin mused, *he'd better come up with the right answer.* Goodwin shook his head. "You knew the answer before you asked it," he said.

"Look what I brought you," Kohora said, reaching into her handbag. She had made two ham sandwiches for Goodwin and smuggled them in. "You can give the IV a rest.

Don't eat both of them now. Save one for later."

When Goodwin saw the sandwiches, he forgot about the IV tubing and almost tipped the stand over reaching for them.

"I'll never complain about the junk you keep in your handbag again," Goodwin said.

He tried to unwrap one of the sandwiches. While Goodwin was busy fumbling with the paper on one of the sandwiches he had grabbed.

"Take this one," Kohora said, handing Goodwin the sandwich she had unwrapped.

Goodwin grabbed the sandwich and bit into it as though he hadn't eaten in a week (it had been almost that long).

"Have they been feeding my baby?" Kohora asked.

Between chewing and swallowing, Goodwin managed to answer. "Yeah. That stuff in that bottle whatever it is." Goodwin wiped his mouth with the napkin that Kohora provided and caught his breath. "Did you come to take me home?"

"No, but I'll stay with you until visiting hours are over. How's that?"

"I'm disappointed," Goodwin answered. "If you stay, that sounds good to me. I'd still like to go home. Now! The two of us can get out of here... Please."

"What did the doctor say?" Kohora asked, shaking her finger at Goodwin.

"Okay, okay, don't get mad."

"I'm not angry. You should relax and accept the fact that you are going to spend the night here. Doctor's orders and mine, too. Ready for your other sandwich?"

"I can wait," Goodwin said with a sparkle in his eyes. "Having you here is worth five or six sandwiches. Pull your chair closer to the bed. Better, come over and sit on the bed."

Looking at her husband suspiciously, Kohora slowly inched her way toward the bed.

Before Kohora could sit on the edge of the bed.

"Slip your shoes off," Goodwin said, reaching out and helping Kohora slide around and putting her feet on the bed. "That's better than hanging them over the side."

"You must promise to control yourself," she said, placing her index finger on

Goodwin's nose and letting it slide down to his lips.

"Scout's honor, dear. I won't try anything."

"I know you Goodwin Phost. When it comes to making out, any halfway secluded place will do."

"You really think. I mean. Really think," Goodwin said, making a cross over his chest.

"I'd do something like that in this room with anyone?"

"If you do, it had better be with me," Kohora replied. "You like women. I knew it when I married you, but you said I would be the only one."

"I flirt a little," Goodwin said, "but you know where my heart is. You have your own little way of flirting, too."

"Of course I flirt with you," Kohora said.

"I can't help it," Goodwin said. "Do you flirt with that Dr. Wells? You work with the guy every day."

"That's right. It's nothing more than a working relationship," Kohora said, moving closer to Goodwin while throwing one of her legs over his leg. "But if I need help with something that might be too heavy, and Dr. Wells is around, I'll turn on the charm."

"I don't know what made me ask that question," Goodwin said, placing his left hand on his wife's lap. "It won't happen again. It must be my hand that caused me to talk stupid like that. Maybe some TLC would help me. You haven't kissed me since you've been here."

"I don't want ham on my lips," Kohora said.

"You aren't jealous of a little old ham sandwich are you?" Goodwin asked.

"No, but you were famished. I didn't want to interrupt you," Kohora said. "Come closer and let me be your dessert." Goodwin leaned closer, and then it happened.

"Not again," Goodwin yelled, jerking his lips away from his wife.

"What did I do?" Kohora asked with an expression of confusion and pain.

"Nothing," Goodwin answered, shaking his head. "I got this sharp pain in my left arm and it went to my chest. Maybe I'm allergic to you."

"You know that old saying, 'it hurt so good'," Kohora said.

Goodwin was silent as he tried to figure out what was happening to him.

"Maybe it was your awkward position," Kohora said as she stood up. She bent over to kiss Goodwin. His left side trembled, causing him to turn away.

Upset by his reaction to Kohora, Goodwin dropped his head. "I don't know what came over me," he said. "I'm not that sick."

"Give me your hand," Kohora said, reaching for the injured hand and began massaging it. "Your hand is heavy. All of the food must go to it." Goodwin had completely relaxed and let the full weight of the hand rest on Kohora's lap.

"Oooh, that feels so good," Goodwin said. "Maybe you can spend the night."

"Darn it, time certainly does pass when you're enjoying yourself," Kohora said looking at her watch. "Do you think I'll be able to get a little sugar before I go?"

"Of course," Goodwin gleefully replied, leaning to his right toward Kohora. "Make it a passionate one."

"Let's sample it first," Kohora said quickly, smacking Goodwin on the cheek and then on the lips. "I think it's safe for the real thing." Kohora parted her lips slightly as she prepared to French kiss her husband.

Goodwin jerked away before their lips came together. "Give me that other sandwich.

I'm ready for it," Goodwin said. *Ow.* He thought. *What's happening to me? I'm not hungry, and it's stupid to think that I'm allergic to Kohora.*

"Here! Take the sandwich," Kohora said. "I'm going home. It's after ten."

What have I done? Goodwin questioned himself. "I'm sorry. Do you have to go?" he asked. "I don't want you to go. I'm in pain at the thought of you leaving. I'm serious honey, don't leave me!"

"I don't want to leave," Kohora said. "But it's time to go."

"I understand what's wrong," Goodwin said. "You're upset because I asked for my other sandwich in the middle of our kiss. I don't know why I did it. Something came over me don't leave. Please stay a little longer."

"Yes I was upset," Kohora said. "What if I preferred food over sex?"

"You wouldn't would you?"

"Just a thought," Kohora replied. "Okay... I'll stay a little longer. Then I must go."

Time in Dr. Midwiff's office; "Do you think Goodwin should be released in the morning?" Dr. Wells asked. "We need to watch him closely."

"If there aren't any more complications, I suppose we'll have to let him go."

"I don't agree with your decision," Dr. Wells said, "I think we should keep him in the hospital for a few more days. We might learn more about his ailment. Do you think Goodwin told us everything?"

"Like what?" Dr. Midwiff asked.

"He could have forgotten something."

"I questioned him myself, and he tried to think of everything that had happened in the last two weeks, but he couldn't remember anything unusual."

"I'm going home," Dr. Wells said, "see you in the morning."

***

Meanwhile, in Goodwin's room, "Honey, it's almost eleven o'clock," Kohora said, "I had better go."

Goodwin was silent. Very slowly, he said, "Okay, but I wish you could stay. I'll miss you." He looked at his lovely wife with a please don't go stare.

"Cheer up. I'll be here early in the morning with a couple of beef sandwiches. How about that? I won't have to smuggle them in, either."

Goodwin smiled a crocodile grin. "That would be great," he said, "but I'm still upset."

His sore hand had begun to vibrate. Kohora got up to leave. Goodwin clutched his left wrist with his right hand as he fell back on the bed in agony.

"Goodwin, Goodwin," Kohora shouted, reaching out to console her husband. She quickly paged Dr. Midwiff.

***

"What happened?" Dr. Midwiff burst through the door to Goodwin's room. A nurse followed closely behind him.

"Goodwin didn't want me to leave, but I didn't think he was that serious about it."

Dr. Midwiff rushed over to Goodwin, who was doubled up in pain and mumbling to himself. Dr. Midwiff placed his hand on Goodwin's left arm. "Easy son, relax. Nurse, get me a sedative." The doctor continued massaging Goodwin's left arm down to his thumb.

"Honey, I won't leave," Kohora said. She placed the IV stand in an upright position.

"I'll stay as long as you want me to."

The nurse returned with the sedative, but Kohora took the syringe from her.

"I'll give it to my h-u-s-b-a-n-d," she said

By this time, Goodwin had settled down and tried to relax. "He'll be okay," Dr.

Midwiff said. "When was the last time that bottle was replaced?"

"Nobody's been in the room since seven-something," Kohora replied.

"I didn't think it was necessary with his wife in here," the nurse said. "All they had to do was call me."

Dr. Midwiff shook his head. "Bring a fresh bottle right away," he said, ushering the nurse out of the room.

"Dr. Midwiff, I'm sorry," Kohora said, feeling somewhat responsible for Goodwin's actions. "I should have left when visiting hours were over. I'll go now."

"Don't. Please don't... don't go," Goodwin pleaded. He lay his head on the pillow and closed his eyes.

"What about the sedative?" Kohora asked. "Should I give it to him?"

"No," Dr. Midwiff answered. "He won't need it, but maybe you had better spend the night here at the hospital."

"Here? All night? Where?"

"In Goodwin's room. I'll have a cot brought in. He shouldn't be left alone. The nurse will be instructed as before; to check and replace Goodwin's IV every hour on the hour, if not sooner."

"Are you sure about my staying the night here?" Kohora asked, hoping Dr. Midwiff hadn't changed his mind.

"Yes. Yes, I am," Dr. Midwiff answered. "It would be good for both of you. Mrs. Phost please step outside with me for a minute." Outside Goodwin's room; "Your husband has been acting strange. Does he have an allergy? Are you two having any problems that might have caused this behavior?"

"Funny you should ask," Kohora replied with a slight smile. "Because lately, it has been as though Goodwin were allergic to me. Problems...? I want a baby, but Goodwin isn't too eager at this time, with him laid off from his job."

"What about his attitude toward the hospital?" Dr. Midwiff asked, trying to determine from Kohora's facial expression if there was a problem.

"Like what?" She asked.

"He doesn't want our help," Dr. Midwiff answered.

"My husband hates hospitals. He hates to be sick. That's why he's always exercising and talking about people who don't." Kohora continued.

"Goodwin told me there wasn't anything he wouldn't stop doing short of making love if a doctor told him it would save his life. My husband loves life and people. I think that's one of the reasons I love him so much."

"I'm impressed," Dr. Midwiff said. "I understand what you mean, Mrs. Phost. If everything goes well tonight, Goodwin will be released in the morning . . ."

"Kohora! Where are you?" Goodwin asked, opening his eyes, looking for his wife.

"Right here, darling," Kohora answered, pushing the door open and sticking her head inside. "Do you need anything?"

"What are you doing out there?"

"Talking to Dr. Midwiff."

"Scheming against me? I suppose."

"Don't be so suspicious," Kohora said. "Dr. Midwiff asked me a few questions about your thumb. He thought maybe I could shed some light on your mysterious injury."

"You had better go in," Dr. Midwiff said, "I'll see you in the morning, if not sooner."

***

Inside Goodwin's room, Kohora went over to him in an attempt to console Goodwin.

"How does that feel?" Kohora asked, rubbing Goodwin's swollen hand. "I thought you'd be asleep by now."

"I couldn't sleep with this damn thing in my arm. What did you expect?"

"I'll rub it until you go to sleep," Kohora said, rubbing Goodwin's hand while she hummed a lullaby.

Goodwin finally went to sleep. A cot was brought into Goodwin's room and Kohora tried to get some sleep, too. She kept her hand on Goodwin's fat hand. Every time Kohora dozed, her hand would slide off Goodwin's hand. Or the nurse would come into the room with a full IV bottle. Goodwin slept for four hours and didn't wake up for food.

***

Friday morning, Kohora and Goodwin went to Dr. Midwiff's office to discuss Goodwin's release. "I guess it'll be okay if you go home this morning," Dr. Midwiff said.

"There isn't much we can do until the results from the tests come back."

"I'm free at last," Goodwin said, "thanks, doc."

"I'll walk you to the car," Kohora said. "Are you sure you'll be able to drive?"

"It'll be rough," Goodwin replied with a grimace, but I'll make it."

"Then I'll get a bite and start my day."

As Kohora and Goodwin neared the exit leading to the outside, Goodwin thought he heard a voice. *You can't leave.* Followed by spasms in his left arm. Goodwin gasped for air. The pain in his arm became intense. Goodwin's steps became shorter until he dragged his feet with each step. Goodwin leaned on Kohora.

"Honey, are you all right?" Kohora asked, sensing a problem.

"I don't know," Goodwin whispered, closing his eyes. "My arm won't stop shaking."

Goodwin crumpled to the floor, blocking one of the exits. Kohora called for help.

An emergency crew came immediately and took Goodwin back to his old room which hadn't been reassigned.

***

When Goodwin regained consciousness, it was as if he hadn't left at all. There was the IV and its connections plus the familiar face of Dr. Midwiff.

"Goodwin, what happened? I thought you'd be home by now," he said.

"I don't know," Goodwin answered. "One minute, I was about to walk out the door and the next thing I knew, I was back in this room looking at you."

"Apparently, you had a relapse," Dr. Midwiff said, "or you passed out for lack of food. At any rate, I'm committed to finding the problem. Relax while I go over your charts again and map out a plan of attack. If you need me, I'll be in my office."

***

It was Saturday morning. "Come in," Dr. Midwiff said as Dr. Wells pushed the door open and stuck his head in.

"Good morning," Dr. Wells said. "Has Goodwin been released?"

"Yes and no," Dr. Midwiff answered. "Yes, he was released, but …"

"But what?"

"Goodwin passed out just as they neared the door to leave. I had Goodwin put in his old room. By the way, Kohora spent the night in Goodwin's room."

"What for?" Dr. Wells asked. "He doesn't deserve Kohora, and he's not a baby."

Dr. Midwiff smiled. "Do I detect a hint of envy?" He asked.

The red-faced Dr. Wells shook his head.

"Good," Dr. Midwiff said. "That's the last thing we would need – a love triangle.

After their misunderstanding, "Kohora didn't want to leave Goodwin in his condition."

"What condition?" Dr. Wells asked. "Is Goodwin okay?"

"He had spasms again," Dr. Midwiff said. The left arm shook and jerked violently."

"Kohora had to stay overnight because of that?" Dr. Wells asked.

"Was there anything wrong with her spending the night with her HUSBAND?"

"No, but I would like to have been there," Dr. Wells replied.

"For what?" Dr. Midwiff asked. "You had better curb your intentions."

Changing the subject, Dr. Wells asked, "What are we going to do about our patient?"

"Not much until the test results come back," Dr. Midwiff replied, "but I'll call you if Goodwin's condition gets worse."

"Is there anything else I should know?" Dr. Wells asked.

Dr. Midwiff ran his hand through his hair. "No, but Goodwin's symptoms have me puzzled. Every time he becomes upset, the hand seems to be directly affected."

Dr. Wells was about to leave, but Dr. Midwiff's last statement caused him to turn around and face his coworker. "Like how?" Dr. Wells asked

"Earlier, Goodwin and Kohora embraced, and the hand went into spasms," Dr. Midwiff explained. "He became angry about something; again, the hand reacted." Dr. Midwiff paused. "This morning, when Goodwin was released and came near the door, the hand responded. Then there's his appetite."

"Whoa. Wait a minute," Dr. Wells said. "All of those events could have been planned or they're just plain coincidences." Dr. Wells gathered his thoughts. "Goodwin wanted Kohora's attention or any woman's attention, the way he struts around in that jogging suit. I'll bet he or Kohora paid good money for it."

"I know you don't like Goodwin, but you're sweet on his wife. If he knew how much, one of them would have to find another place to work."

"What can I say?" Dr. Wells asked with a smirk. "Back to what you said about the hand. How do we prove the connection between what you said and the real reason?"

"I have a plan," Dr. Midwiff said, following the statement with a yawn and a stretch.

"Maybe we could simulate certain conditions and see if the hand responds."

"Sounds good to me," Dr. Wells said, "when do we start? If Goodwin finds out, what do think he'd do? He might leave the hospital anytime."

"We could do the test now," Dr. Midwiff answered, "or in the next hour. I don't think Goodwin is going anywhere soon. We should keep him overnight. At least until we've had a chance to play our little game with his hand."

"It's almost ten a.m.. We had better get over to Goodwin's room and give him the bad news."

***

Dr. Midwiff and Dr. Wells entered Goodwin's room just as the nurse replaced his empty IV bottle. "Good Morning, Mr. Phost," Dr. Midwiff said, "having an early lunch or a late breakfast?"

"What's this, Mr. Phost b.s.?" Goodwin shook his head. "Look out, Mr. P-h-o-s-t."

Goodwin mocked Dr. Midwiff. "The shafters are here. The nurse brought me a full bottle, so it's neither. I don't think of that liquid junk as food?"

"I hope we didn't disturb you," Dr. Midwiff said. "Dr. Wells and I have a plan that might help us to help you."

"And what could that be?" Goodwin asked casting a wary eye at both of the doctors.

"Let me guess. I can go home?"

Both doctors dropped their heads, feigning disappointment. "You had better handle this," Dr. Wells said.

Dr. Midwiff studied Goodwin's facial expression. How could he soften the impact of what he was about to say. He took a deep breath. "Goodwin." Dr. Midwiff paused.

The suspense got to Goodwin. "Out with it, doc," Goodwin shouted, "I've been up that trail before. I'll survive."

"Try to understand where I'm coming from," Dr. Midwiff continued. "Everything we do is for your benefit."

"Say what you have to say because I'm leaving."

"No," Dr. Midwiff said as firmly as he could. "We need you here one more night."

"What are you saying?" Goodwin asked, leaping out of the bed, forgetting about the hospital gown he was wearing and the IV connections. "Whose idea was it?" Goodwin looked directly at Dr. Wells.

Dr. Wells shook his head vigorously. "Dr. Midwiff is your doctor," he said. "Dr. Midwiff kept me on because of the peculiarities of your case. I follow his instructions."

"Now, now, Mr. Phost," Dr. Midwiff said. "Don't be upset. We only want to help you and we can't do it if you are at home."

"I should be at home," Goodwin said, inhaling deeply. "I'll never recover in this place.

If my case is so strange, why don't you get somebody older than him?" Goodwin pointed and shook his finger at Dr. Wells. "He's not as old as I am."

"Dr. Wells is an expert in genetic engineering."

"I've heard that before too many times."

"You haven't heard our proposal yet," Dr. Wells said, breaking into the conversation.

"Don't you want to hear it?"

"Yes, I'll hear it when you call me at home. I'm leaving."

"I see," Dr. Wells said. "You're going to eat and run." Dr. Wells began to laugh.

"That's part of the problem. I'm being starved to death. I wouldn't have passed out if I were fed properly. My appetite is great."

"Okay, okay," Dr. Midwiff said. "I think you can have solid food." He waited for Goodwin's reaction. "Won't you stay until we have time to evaluate the test results? If we're satisfied, you can leave."

"And if you're not pleased, then what?"

Dr. Midwiff considered the question before he answered. "We'll let you decide."

"But Dr. Midwiff," Dr. Wells broke in. "I thought…"

Dr. Midwiff shook his head and waved his hand. "It's his body. What can we do?"

"Thanks, doc. I'll put my clothes on so when you and Dr. Wells reach a conclusion,

I'll be ready to get out of this place."

"Dr. Midwiff, please report to your office. Dr. Midwiff, please report to your…" the voice on the loudspeaker barked.

"The test results must be in. I'll be right back."

***

"Dr. Midwiff returned to Goodwin's room, bringing the test results and Nicia Ling, the lab technician with him. Apprehensively, "Here they are," Dr. Midwiff said, waving the large manila envelope in Dr. Wells' direction. "This should tell us something. Nicia, I believe you know Mr. Phost."

"It's Goodwin, doc," Goodwin said, correcting Dr. Wells. "Hello, Nicia."

"Hello, Goodwin. How are you?" Nicia asked.

"Feeling better now and you?"

Somewhat nervous because of Goodwin's openness, "I'm fine," Nicia replied.

"Relax, Nicia. You're among friends," Goodwin said.

Dr. Midwiff opened the envelope that contained the test results they had waited for.

"We'll go to my office and take a look," he said. "Our patient wouldn't be interested in medical jargon would you?"

"You're so right, doc. That's a good idea. Nicia can keep me company."

"Only if you behave yourself," Dr. Wells said, shaking his index finger at Goodwin.

"Don't worry about me," Goodwin said. *I remember what happens when I try to kiss my wife.* Goodwin recalled.

***

They left and went to Dr. Midwiff's office, where he read the report aloud to Dr. Wells.

The report: **"The fluoroscopic picture of the thumb revealed a strange object that looked like the beginning of a bean sprout. We've never seen anything like this before. We could not determine if the object is the whole as it is or part of something that will get much larger, or will it retain its present form if and when it reaches its full growth. If it doesn't get any larger, you might be able to amputate it.**

Please keep us up to date on any changes that might occur."

"I wonder what they meant by, 'whether the object is the whole or part of something that will get bigger and change its shape." Dr. Midwiff said.

"One thing that comes to mind," Dr. Wells said. "Take a bean, for example. The adult plant doesn't look anything like a bean. We also look a lot different from our beginning to the finished product. What does the EKG report reveal?"

Dr. Midwiff took the report from its envelope and read it. The report: **"We have another problem. There was an extra line on the screen. It could have been a murmur, echo, or some kind of harmonic that was superimposed on the major one"**

Dr. Midwiff stopped reading and said, "I don't believe this."

Dr. Wells stared back at Dr. Midwiff with a look of amazement. "Please continue," he said, followed by a hand gesture.

Dr. Midwiff shook his head. **"But it is entirely possible that it could be an extra heartbeat. Based on what we found after analyzing the fluid you sent us, we are almost certain that it is some kind of rhythmic phenomenon, if it isn't an extra heartbeat."** Thrusting the report at Dr. Wells, "Here! You read the rest of this..." Dr. Midwiff said giving the report to Dr. Wells.

Dr. Wells eagerly took the report and began to read. **"We hope you made a mistake and got that sample mixed up with fluid from a pregnant woman. What we're trying to say is; there must have been a mix-up somewhere. The fluid has all the properties of the amniotic fluid that protect a fetus in its mother's womb. But if it came from where you said it did, you might have a very dangerous parasite on your hands. There's not much we can do. Maybe if the situation got worse, you could have the patient flown back here to us, or if that wasn't possible, one of us could fly out there. This could turn out to be quite exciting."**

"The section about amniotic fluid," Dr. Midwiff said. "That's odd."

Dr. Wells smiled.

"What's so funny?" Dr. Midwiff asked.

"This is hypothetical," Dr. Wells said, "but you've heard of spontaneous combustion.

This could very well be a similar phenomenon."

"Yes, I have," the perplexed Dr. Midwiff said. "What exactly are you getting at?"

"I'd have to call Goodwin's condition a form of **spontaneous embryogenesis,**" Dr. Wells said with an even larger grin than before.

"What are you saying?" the still perplexed Dr. Midwiff asked. "But Goodwin isn't pregnant. Don't repeat this to anyone else, but how do we tell Goodwin that he can't leave the hospital?"

Dr. Wells looked at his watch. "It's close to lunchtime. The bad news will have to wait. I'm sure Goodwin will be glad to see the food. The cook down in the kitchen told me that he had been sending food to Goodwin's room between regular mealtimes. They must have a hell of a grocery bill."

***

Back in Goodwin's room, "I'll leave and let you enjoy your lunch," Licia said.

"You don't have to go," Goodwin said. "Why don't you bring your lunch in here and have lunch with me? I've behaved myself haven't I?"

Before Nicia could answer, "Nicia, it's lunchtime," Dr. Wells said, sticking his head through the door. "Are you coming?"

Smiling as though she had pulled a fast one, Nicia said, "See you later, Goodwin."

After Goodwin finished his hearty lunch (extra portions, thanks to Kohora), he pushed the rolling stand with the empty tray to one side, leaned back on the bed, and closed his eyes. *That wasn't bad for hospital food,* Goodwin thought. He looked at his fat left hand and stifled a yawn. *I feel good. Except for my swollen hand, there's nothing wrong with me. Why should I stay in this place and let them experiment on me? Why didn't Wells or Midwiff tell me what was on those reports from back East or where ever they sent them? I'll get dressed and wait for them. Maybe they'll come and tell me what's on those reports. Why should I wait? The weather is fine and my jogging suit is going to waste. That was some lunch.* Goodwin rubbed his stomach. *That's why I passed out. I haven't had any real food. There's no reason for me to stay. I'm leaving!*

***

Dr. Wells, Dr. Midwiff, and Licia, the lab technician, sat in the break area having lunch.

"Nicia, we have the lab report from back East," Dr. Midwiff said, "care to look at it?"

Nicia breathed deeply and shook her head. "Is everything okay?" she asked.

"Yes," Dr. Midwiff replied. "I hope you weren't offended because we double-checked your findings, but we had to be sure. The results were the same." Dr. Midwiff let out a sigh of relief. "Goodwin's infection or whatever it is, has gotten worse."

"Dr. Midwiff, I understand," Nicia said with a renewed look of self-confidence. "I didn't want to believe the results that I came up with. I was hoping for Goodwin's sake, that I was wrong."

The two doctors nodded in agreement. "But as fate would have it," Dr. Midwiff said.

"No such luck."

"Something positive may come from this," Dr. Wells said, rubbing his hands together.

"It'll give me a chance to apply some of my specialized genetics training. Whatever it is, I'm sure I can stop it. I'm excited about the whole thing."

"How can you talk like that when a man's life might be in jeopardy?" Dr. Midwiff asked with a slight frown on his face. "I know you don't like the man, but you don't have to rejoice at his misfortune."

"I'm not rejoicing," Dr. Wells quickly added, "but as I said before, this could turn out to be quite an event . . . I could become famous, and Goodwin would be cured. That would be quite a feat." Dr. Wells' enthusiasm got the best of him. "Goodwin might not like me any better, but Kohora would adore me."

Nicia knew her coworker better than Dr. Wells did. "She would be grateful," Nicia said. She looked at Dr. Wells as though they were the only ones at the table. "But she loves Goodwin."

"Don't be angry with me," Dr. Wells said, trying to ignore what Nicia had said. "I've seen how Goodwin looks at you, but you're only interested in your work. Such a lovely young lady. Maybe you like him more than you would care to admit."

Annoyed by Dr. Wells' statement, Nicia said, "When I'm ready, I'll choose who I want to go out with and it won't be you."

Dr. Midwiff sat through the verbal sockfest as if he were the father watching his kids abuse each other with words. "That's enough," Dr. Midwiff finally said. "We have a very sick patient who needs our undivided attention. We had better get back to his room and give him the bad news and I don't mean the lab report. We can't let Goodwin leave the hospital. Are you coming with us, Miss Ling?"

"You don't need me now. I had better get back to the lab."

"I disagree," Dr. Wells said, "you might be just what we need. You keep Goodwin and I'm honest. Besides, Goodwin would be more cooperative with your pretty face around and you'd take my mind off Kohora."

Nicia ignored Dr. Wells' last statement and got up to leave. "I think you should come with us," Dr. Midwiff said. "We might need your help."

"What you need is a nurse," Nicia said. "If you need a woman, call Kohora."

"We need two women," Dr. Midwiff said, smiling. "Both of you will take part in this experiment. Kohora will enjoy her part, but you won't enjoy your part and neither will Kohora."

"Dr. Midwiff, I don't understand," Nicia said. "What will I have to do in this experiment?"

"Wait and see," Dr. Midwiff replied. "We had better get back to Goodwin's room. He might decide to leave again."

***

A few feet from Goodwin's room, they saw him leaving. When Goodwin saw them, he turned and went in the opposite direction. "Hold it, Goodwin. Where do you think you're going?" Dr. Wells shouted, moving quickly in an effort to overtake Goodwin.

"You can't leave now. Not when we have a test that might give us some answers that will Help solve the mystery of your swollen hand."

Goodwin slowed his pace, but continued to walk away from them. Dr. Midwiff and Nicia joined Dr. Wells in the pursuit.

Goodwin glanced over his shoulder and saw them gaining on him. Goodwin walked faster and the distance between them increased. *If I can make it to the next corner,* he thought. *I can lose them. What's happening to me? I hope it's not another one of those attacks. My arm is killing me. But I can still make it to the corner. My legs . . . what's wrong with them?* Goodwin stumbled and went to his knees, and the rest of his body followed. Goodwin crumpled to the floor.

"Goodwin!" Nicia shouted, breaking away from the two doctors. Nicia leaned over the hapless Goodwin. Her dark eyes filled with concern.

Dr. Wells bent over Goodwin, checked his pulse, and pulled one of his eyelids back.

"He's okay," Dr. Wells said. "Just another fainting spell."

"That's the second or third time Goodwin has fainted since he's been here," Dr. Midwiff said. "There's more to his illness than he realized. Call an attendant and get Goodwin went back to his room."

***

Goodwin sat up in his bed with a subdued look on his face. "Why are you guys looking at me? What did I do?"

"Put this on," Kohora said, handing Goodwin a hospital gown. "That jogging suit looked out of place. I hope you won't try another one of your great escapes."

Goodwin kept his head down. "I've learned something," he said reaching for the gown. "What chance do I have? You and those two doctors are against me. Nicia, where do you stand?"

Nicia shook her head. "I'm not in this whatever it is," she said.

"Kohora, please pull the curtain so I can change," Goodwin said. "I'll stay until this mystery is solved." After a few minutes, "you can open the curtain now. How do I look?"

"Like a patient," everyone exclaimed.

"More like a prisoner. I'm beginning to feel like one, too," Goodwin said. "What did the test results show?"

Not a word was spoken. Everyone looked at each other.

"Was it that bad?" Goodwin asked. "If you want me to stay, you better tell me or I'll leave first chance I get."

"It's not up to you," Dr. Wells said with a tone of decisiveness. He pointed at Goodwin's left hand. "That hand is infected, and it could be hazardous to your health."

"The news isn't that bad," Dr. Midwiff said, motioning for Dr. Wells. "You'll live, but you aren't out of the woods yet."

"I don't need a long speech," Goodwin said. "Get to the point. The sooner you do, the quicker I can get out of this place."

"Let me explain the circumstances to Mr. Phost," Dr. Midwiff said with an air of authority.

Angrily, the ambitious Dr. Wells said, "I thought you were going to let me explain the results to Goodwin." I'm the expert in this field."

"That's enough, Wells," Dr. Midwiff said.

"That's right. Wells," Goodwin said. "Let me hear what Dr. Midwiff has to say. He sounds very professional. You sound more like you're gloating."

"Don't be so hard on Dr. Wells," Kohora said. "He's just as concerned about your as Dr. Midwiff is healthy, but he's more enthusiastic; whereas, Dr. Midwiff is more . . . settled and used to strange ailments."

"If I may continue . . ." Dr. Midwiff said, stepping closer to Goodwin as if he were going to whisper in his ear. "We've discovered a growth on your thumb that has grown larger than we had anticipated."

"Do you think it'll get much bigger?" Goodwin asked, looking at his hand as though he had just discovered it.

"Mr. Phost, let me continue," Dr. Midwiff said. "We have detected what seems to be an extra, but faint heartbeat. The fluoroscopic image of the thumb revealed what looked like a pinto bean sprouting upside down where your thumb used to be."

Goodwin held his swollen hand at arm's length, then brought it closer as he stared at it. "Is there something I haven't been told ?" Goodwin asked. "Is it cancer? Why are all of you looking at me like that?"

"Like what?" Kohora asked.

"You know," Goodwin answered, mocking their strained expressions. "You might as well tell me. What are my chances of surviving? Will you have to operate?"

"Mr. Phost, as I said earlier, it's not serious. More puzzling than anything else. With the symptoms you've had and the fainting spells." Dr. Midwiff paused.

"What are you leading up to?" Goodwin asked. "Anybody can faint."

"It's not just the fainting," Dr. Wells said. "The nausea and the craving for food."

"I'm known for my great appetite. As for the nausea, I can't explain. Maybe I ate too much or too fast. Once I leave here, I'll be okay."

"That's not all, Mr. Phost," Dr. Midwiff said. "The fluid from your thumb."

Tell me, doc," Goodwin interrupted. "What about it? Is it water, pus or some rare blood that I can sell and get rich?"

Moving toward Goodwin and placing her arm around his shoulder. "Honey," Kohora said. "Let Dr. Midwiff finish."

"Okay, Midwiff, let me have it.'

Dr. Midwiff looked at the report, then at Goodwin. After a long minute. "The fluid;

This is hard," he said.

"What about the fluid?" Goodwin asked.

"Let me tell him," Dr. Wells volunteered.

"Everybody, calm down," Dr. Midwiff said. "Mr. Phost. Please don't be offended by what I'm about to say." Dr. Midwiff shuffled the report between his thumb and fore-finger. "The fluid has the same chemical makeup as the amniotic fluid that surrounds the fetus in a pregnant woman."

Silence fell over the room like a curtain had been drawn, signaling the end of a dramatic scene in a live play. Goodwin stared straight ahead as if he were trying to look through the wall. He continued to stare like a man who had suddenly lost his eyesight and was trying to look past the darkness. Kohora turned and looked at her husband, but didn't say anything.

This man has to be crazy. Goodwin thought. *I know I shouldn't have come here. Look at them. They don't know what to say or do. I know what I'm going to do. When they leave, I'm leaving.* Finally, Goodwin spoke, "It's not every day that a man is told that he's pregnant."

"We know you're not pregnant, Darling," Kohora said, stroking the back of Goodwin's neck and laughing. "That's the last thing you'd want to happen. It might ruin your chances for a career. I'm the one who wants to get pregnant."

The others laughed at Kohora's joke, but Goodwin looked at her and said, "Now that my secret is out, should I opt for an abortion?"

"No," Kohora said, vigorously shaking her head. "Besides, I want a baby."

The mockery continued. "But it's my body," Goodwin said. "I have that right, or is it for women only?"

"Let's be serious about this," Dr. Midwiff said. "We might have to operate."

Suddenly, Goodwin's left hand began to shake as he grabbed it, simulating a one-on-one arm wrestling exhibition. Kohora continued to stroke the back of Goodwin's neck.

"Dr. Midwiff, do something," Kohora said.

When he grabbed Goodwin's left arm, "Midwiff, do something," Goodwin yelled.

"Do something about this pain."

"Call the nurse," Dr. Midwiff said, "Have her bring me a painkiller."

The struggle went on, with Kohora flailing about as she tried to hang onto Goodwin's neck. Dr. Wells rushed over to help restrain Goodwin's legs. Nicia went to the nurse.

"Here's the painkiller and a sedative," the nurse said, bursting through the door, waving the hypodermic needle in the air.

"You guys hold Goodwin," Kohora said, "I'll give him the injection."

At the sight of the needle, Goodwin sent Dr. Midwiff and Dr. Wells sprawling to the floor. "Don't stick me with that needle!" Goodwin said. He tried to be calm. "The pain has stopped. Just bring me some food." Goodwin was standing by the bed. He looked at the two doctors who were trying to figure out what had happened. Goodwin held onto his left hand.

"Get some food in here," Dr. Midwiff ordered. He straightened his clothes and caught his breath. "Are you sure you want to eat? Calm down first."

"What did I say?" Goodwin asked with a scowl. "I'm hungry. Either I'm not getting enough to eat or there's too much time between meals."

"That's another peculiarity about your ailment," Dr. Midwiff said, "your appetite might be good, but this goes beyond an appetite."

"Tell'em, Honey. Tell'em what a good appetite I have," Goodwin said, appealing to his wife to back up his statement.

"You do have quite an appetite," Kohora said, "but lately it has become voracious.

You've always eaten a lot, but not so often."

"I can't help it if I'm hungry."

"How many times have you eaten today?" Kohora asked in a concerned tone. "They always bring extra portions."

"Mealtime," the food server announced as she entered the room. "Is there some kind of party is going on?"

"A party of one," a perturbed Goodwin answered. "Just do your job and leave."

After Goodwin finished another hearty meal, he was more than willing to cooperate with Dr. Midwiff and Dr. Wells.

"Okay, doc," Goodwin said. He looked directly at Dr. Midwiff. "What shall I do?"

"We would like to examine your hand again," Dr. Wells said, "after which we have a little experiment to perform."

"Like what?!" Goodwin asked, perking up and focusing his gaze on Dr. Wells. "Okay, as long as you don't have to stick me or cut me."

"No," Dr. Wells replied. "This experiment will determine if the hand is sensitive to external stimuli."

"You're wasting my time. I'll be out of here by tonight. I don't plan on being here any longer than I have to."

"Does this hurt?" Dr. Midwiff asked while he squeezed the exaggerated form that was used to be Goodwin's thumb. Dr. Midwiff continued to manipulate the bubble that had replaced Goodwin's thumb. "It's spongy, yet it's tough." Dr. Midwiff gave the bubble a bone-crunching squeeze.

"Stop him!" The voice inside of Goodwin's head said. "What the hell are you doing?"

Goodwin asked Dr. Midwiff as he clutched his arm in agony.

"Where does it hurt?" Dr. Midwiff asked.

"All over, man. From that dome at the top," Goodwin answered, "clear up to my armpit. Goodwin ran his right hand up and down his left arm as if he were scratching an insatiable itch.

Having released his grip on the bubble, Dr. Midwiff asked, "Does it still hurt?"

"No, "Goodwin answered, "since you stopped crushing it."

"I thought you said it wasn't sore."

"It wasn't until you attacked it," Goodwin replied.

"May I take a look at it?" Dr. Wells asked. Goodwin snatched his swollen hand back before Dr. Wells had finished talking.

"Honey, let him see it. Dr. Wells is working on your case, too."

"Just a reflex," Goodwin said. He offered his swollen hand to the dejected Dr. Wells.

Dr. Wells gently took Goodwin's hand. "It's larger today than it was yesterday." Dr.

Wells said, "Not a lot, but noticeable."

"We had better get on with our performance test." Dr. Midwiff said, motioning for Kohora is to come closer for instructions. "You'll be first, Mrs. Phost. Here's what I want you to do. Kiss your husband! Then hug him and let him caress you. We can leave the room if you want us to."

"That won't be necessary," Kohora said, going over and giving Goodwin a long passionate kiss on his lips, and her tongue slides down to his chin. She put her arms around him and made sure her breasts pressed against him. Goodwin twitched, but did not return the gesture.

Dr. Midwiff frowned. "Mr. Phost!" He said. "Don't sit there. Kiss her back."

Goodwin looked at Dr. Midwiff, then at Dr. Wells and Nicia. "What does this have to do with my hand?" The puzzled Goodwin asked. "I don't have time for foolish games."

Somewhat surprised by her husband's lack of response, Kohora asked. "Don't I excite you anymore?"

"It's not a game, Mr. Phost." Dr. Midwiff said. "Kiss, hug, and caress your wife!"

Goodwin thought about it. *The last time I was romantic, I almost had a heart attack.*

"Come on, dear. Kiss me. Touch me. Make me yours," Kohora insisted while she continued rubbing Goodwin's chest. Kohora purred and blew in his ear.

Goodwin closed his eyes and covered them with his good hand. *I don't want the pain.*

The last time I was loving with you, I paid for it. My body wants to respond, but my mind tells me otherwise. Finally, "Honey, I don't see the point."

Angry, "Goodwin Phost, what's come over you?" Kohora asked. She took Goodwin's right hand and tried to put it inside her blouse.

Oh no! Goodwin thought. *I haven't felt this hot since I was a teenager on my first date. I could take my wife and…*

"Come on, Goodwin." Dr. Wells said. "Show us some of that charm that made the lady fall for you."

Kohora kissed Goodwin's eyelids, cheeks, and earlobe while whispering, "I love you.

Do you love me?"

Goodwin grabbed Kohora with his good hand and pulled her closer. "You used to tell me that I lusted after you. Baby. I'm lusting now," Goodwin said.

Kohora gasped for air. "Easy, big boy. That's more like it," she said.

Dr. Midwiff's face turned pink. "Maybe we should leave the room."

The pounding in Goodwin's chest was so loud, it seemed to drown his thoughts. *I know they can hear my heart beating,* he mused. *What can I do? I want to make love to my wife now.* Like water bursting through a weakened dam, Goodwin's passion got the best of him. With his left arm dangling at his side, Goodwin held the limp Kohora up to prevent her from falling. Kohora laid a big kiss on Goodwin's lips, and they remained in that position for a good minute.

"That was quite a kiss," the red-faced Dr. Midwiff said, looking at Dr. Wells and Nicia who were caught up in the passionate performance. Kohora and Goodwin remained entwined until the clapping of hands made them aware that they were not alone.

"Did I pass the test?" Goodwin asked. "Can I leave this place? After a kiss like that, if

I was sick, I'm cured now."

"Not so fast, Mr. Phost," Dr. Midwiff said. "There are two more tests for you to pass.

If you pass those, there wouldn't be any reason to keep you overnight."

"I'm tired of these games," Goodwin said, "but if it'll get me out of here, why not?

What's next, Midwiff?"

"There were actually three more tests," Dr. Midwiff said, "but since the first one was negative, we'll omit the third one."

"Mrs. Phost, hand me one of those hypodermic needles the nurse brought in earlier. I would like to try something."

"He doesn't need a sedative," Kohora said, reaching into her pocket and giving Dr. Midwiff the hypodermic needle.

"I'm not going to give your husband an injection," Dr. Midwiff explained, "but I am going to pretend to do so. Mr. Phost, let me see your swollen hand."

"No way, doc."

"Come on," Dr. Wells pleaded. He reached for Goodwin's hand. "You could be on your way home . . . soon."

Goodwin's left hand shot forward.

"Easy does it, Mr. Phost," Dr. Midwiff said. gripping the needle tightly to prevent it from being knocked from his hand. "Give me your hand." He took Goodwin's swollen hand and held it firmly in his left hand and prepared to pierce it with the needle. Goodwin became tense and tried to pull his hand away, but Dr. Midwiff held it firmly. He brought the needle moved closer and closer to Goodwin's left arm. Sweat had begun to pour from Goodwin's forehead.

"If you wanted to know how I felt about needles," Goodwin said, grabbing Dr. Midwiff's hand. "You could've asked me. I don't like needles hospitals either."

"Let my arm go," Dr. Midwiff said. "This part of the experiment is important."

"Drop the needle, doc. Don't make me hurt you."

Dr. Midwiff continued to bring the needle toward Goodwin's arm.

"Doc, don't let me have to say it again," Goodwin repeated.

"Honey," Kohora interrupted. "Let Dr. Midwiff finish."

"No, I won't. I'm tired of being probed and poked."

"Will you let me do it?" Kohora asked.

Goodwin shook his head. "I don't care who does it, I don't want it done."

"It must be done," Dr. Wells said. He walked over to Goodwin and jerked Goodwin's right hand from Dr. Midwiff's arm.

"Stay out of this, Wells, if you want to be around to practice medicine."

Goodwin cursed and kicked as the two doctors attempted to restrain him.

"Don't hurt him," Kohora said. "If you must hold him, let me do the needlework."

Kohora moved the needle toward the swollen hand as Goodwin continued to struggle.

"Mr. Phost, if you don't stop struggling, I'll have to give you something to calm you down," Dr. Midwiff said. "Relax, I'm not going to stick you with the needle. I want to slide it along the surface of your arm."

"Let me do it," Kohora said. "Maybe Goodwin will calm down."

"Not if you're going to stick me with that needle."

Dr. Midwiff handed the syringe to Kohora. "Just touch the bubble. Don't puncture the skin," he said.

When the needle was within a hair's breadth of Goodwin's thumb, the left hand shook violently. Dr. Midwiff lost his grip. Goodwin was like a man possessed. His right arm pulled away from Dr. Wells, leaving the doctor holding air. Kohora dropped the needle.

"Honey, don't blame the doctors. They had to find out what your reaction would be."

Goodwin was quiet. He sat on the bed holding his left wrist and staring into space.

During the commotion, Nicia stood outside the door and assured everyone that things were under control. Someone called a couple of male nurses.

"We might have found out what the problem was," Dr. Wells said. "It's in his mind."

"Are you saying I'm crazy?" Goodwin asked, giving Dr. Wells the evil eye. "There's nothing wrong with me that the right care or medicine won't fix. Like, getting out of here or some good ole antibiotics."

Dr. Midwiff shook his head. "We can't prescribe anything until we know exactly what your ailment is."

Goodwin rubbed the bubble on his left hand. "What more do you need to know? My hand looks like hell, and my thumb has disappeared. It's simple to me."

"We did confirm one of our suspicions," Dr. Wells said in a satisfactory tone.

Goodwin frowned. "Which was what?" He asked.

"Your hand reacted to the needle," Dr. Wells answered.

Goodwin smiled. "That was probably a knee-jerk reflex on my part."

"Look at your appetite?" Dr. Wells said. "You're constantly eating. You passed out when fluid was drawn from your thumb. It was hard to steady the hand for the X-ray.

You've passed out a number of times while trying to leave the hospital."

"Wait a minute," Goodwin interrupted. "What's that got to do with my hand?"

"You could have a parasite," Dr. Wells said, "it's feeding on your body. As it feeds, it grows. Your hand and thumb are the starting points."

"Parasites can enter the body in a number of ways," Dr. Midwiff said. "If this is what happened to you, we've got to figure out how to attack it without endangering your life."

"Sounds good to me, doc. I was beginning to think you didn't care."

In his best concerned professional tone. "But we do," Dr. Wells said, "That's why you'll have to spend tonight at the hospital."

"What will that prove?"

"Who knows?" Dr. Midwiff said, "So prepare yourself mentally for one more night with us. If you want your wife to stay in the room with you, it's okay. I understand. I'm on duty tonight. I'll be a page away if you need me. Have a good night. Kohora, take care of our star patient. See you in the morning."

Dr. Midwiff left and went to the waiting room, where he would doze off and on until he was called into service.

CHAPTER 7

Early Sunday morning, "Honey! Honey!" Goodwin shouted. "I'm going to stop eating. Look at my hand. The more I eat, the bigger it gets. When I was a kid, my mother would say, 'Goodwin, you must have a worm in you. You eat enough for two people and I can't see where it's going.' If Mother could see me now, she'd see where it went."

"What is it, Goodwin?" The sleepy Kohora asked. "Has the swelling gone down"?

"You didn't hear one word I said. Does this look like it went down? Goodwin thrust his swollen hand toward Kohora, almost punching her in the face. "One meal for me today. This thing has to be starved. Get Dr. Midwiff in here. I want something done about this hand." Kohora paged Dr. Midwiff.

***

Dr. Midwiff responded right away, with Dr. Wells tagging along.

"Here we are, Darling," Kohora said. She ushered the two doctors into the room as though they were being introduced on stage. "You get two for the price of one."

"Come right in," Goodwin said. He pulled his remaining pant leg up. "I'm ready to go home at last."

"I only needed one of you to release me from this... Sickening den of starvation."

"Are you hungry?" Dr. Wells asked. "I'm sure our grocery bill will go down when you leave. But, before you go, we would like to take one more look at your hand."

Goodwin flinched. "You don't have to look at it," he said, placing his right hand over it and rubbing it. "My hand is fine. It might be a little smaller."

"That's not what. . . " Kohora said with an oops! "I want you to get well. Please let them see your hand."

Goodwin continued rubbing his swollen hand where the doctors couldn't get a good look at it. "Am I free to go, or do I just leave?" He asked.

"Mr. Phost. You are free to go," Dr. Midwiff said, "but before you go, allow us the courtesy of looking at your hand one more time. We might have to operate."

"Operate for what?" Goodwin asked. He clutched his left hand tighter as though Dr. Midwiff might take it away from him. Goodwin stared at Kohora. "Tell me you didn't know anything about this."

"No," she answered, looking at Dr. Midwiff. "I would have told you. Is it that serious?

What are you going to do? . . . Amputate?"

"No way," Goodwin interrupted. "I'm keeping my hand."

"I can't say how serious it is." Dr. Midwiff answered, "But it's growing, and who knows how much larger it'll get. At most, we would clip the bubble off. Then we could get at the root of the problem."

Goodwin listened. "Don't I have anything to say about this?" He asked.

"Of course you do," Dr. Midwiff answered. "That's why we're talking. "We need your input before we come to any conclusion. We won't operate unless we are absolutely sure.

Get another opinion if you want, but we've already sent our findings to a couple of the best labs in the country."

"What about it, Wells?" Goodwin asked, looking directly at the doctor. "It wouldn't matter to you if they chopped my whole arm off would it?"

"Maybe this will surprise you," Dr. Wells said, "but I disagree with Dr. Midwiff. I don't think an operation would be the proper thing to do at this time. We might be able to do it with medication. There's a new drug called interferon. It shows great promise in the fight against cancer. Maybe we can use it here."

Surprised and disturbed, Goodwin asked. "Do I have cancer--? Or did you make a mistake in your diagnosis?"

Mr. Phost," Dr. Midwiff said. "The truth is, we don't know exactly what's wrong with your hand. Now, may we examine it?"

Goodwin shook his head. "You have the test results; x-rays, blood samples, and no telling what else you've done. What's the point?"

"Goodwin Phost! Don't be so stubborn," Kohora said. "Let them examine your hand so you can be discharged."

His attitude softened by Kohora's statement, "Go ahead and take a look," Goodwin said, thrusting his hand at Dr. Midwiff. "I suppose you'll look the bubble off."

"I'll take it," Dr. Wells said, intercepting Goodwin's hand before it reached Dr. Midwiff. Dr. Wells gently pressed the palm of the swollen hand and lightly touched the bubble. "I've never seen anything like it. It's rather exciting. If interferon works, we can write about it in one of the leading medical journals. When shall I start the treatments?"

"The board will have to approve it." Dr. Midwiff said.

No, not again. Goodwin thought. I'm hungry. *I won't eat – if it kills me. What am I saying? The way I like food and hate the thought of dying, I must be losing my mind. I won't eat breakfast . . . maybe I'll eat lunch.*

"Are you okay?" Kohora asked. "Is something bothering you? Goodwin!"

"Huh? I'm sorry, Honey," Goodwin said. "What did you say?"

"You had a pained expression on your face," Kohora said, mimicking Goodwin.

"You looked so…"

"So what?" Goodwin asked.

"Maybe Goodwin is hungry," Dr. Wells said. "It's almost eleven o'clock."

"I'm not hungry, but I would like to spend some time alone with my wife. There are decisions to be made."

"We understand." Dr. Midwiff said, and they left.

***

Goodwin grabbed his left arm. *Those damned pains have come back. Dr. Wells was right. I am hungry, but I've been hungry before. In another hour, it'll be lunchtime. Got to make it to lunchtime. Then on to dinnertime, and that's what I'm shooting for.*

"Goodwin!" Kohora said putting her hand on his knee. "We were supposed to talk.

You haven't said a word since they left. Are you sure everything is all right?"

"Sorry Honey," Goodwin said. His thoughts returned to the present. "I hate the idea of spending another night here."

"Once the treatments start," Kohora said. "You might be able to go home."

Goodwin was silent again. His right hand followed the pain. First, to his left shoulder, then down to the left side of his chest and down through his bicep. Goodwin's right hand followed the tingling, which continued through his forearm and into his sore hand alternating from left shoulder to swollen hand, like two little men on either end battling to rip out his arteries or veins. Goodwin was lost in a forced game of tug-of-war.

Kohora laughed. "What are you doing?" She asked.

Forcing a smile, Goodwin answered. "Scratching my itch. What did you think I was doing? And it's not funny."

Goodwin closed his eyes and clenched his teeth. *Kohora must never know.* He slipped his aching hand underneath his thigh. Eyes still closed.

Kohora watched with anxiety. "Are you sleepy?" She asked.

In a guttural tone. "No, I don't want to... Maybe I am. We can talk when I wake up."

"Okay, dear. I have things to do. Are you sure you'll be okay?"

"Yes. Now will you go?"

Kohora got up to leave. "Is there anything I can bring you?" She asked.

Goodwin opened his eyes and grinned. "When you go home this afternoon, you could bring me a couple of your luscious ham sandwiches like those you brought yesterday."

"Is that all?"

"For now, I guess it is."

"What about your razor and a change of clothes – like some PJs?"

"Bring them if you want, but I won't be here that long."

"If we don't stop talking, I'm never going to leave," Kohora said, leaning over and kissing Goodwin on the forehead.

***

Left alone, Goodwin pondered his fate. He hopped out the bed, grabbed his left arm and squeezed it from his elbow to the wrist, trying to ease the pain. Goodwin gritted his teeth and grunted. He paced back and forth around his bed, closed his eyes, and cursed, but the pain didn't go away.

Goodwin reflected on his condition. *Am I glad nobody's here? I can take the pain better if I move around. Like when I was a kid and had to pee. As long as I could wiggle,*

I could hold it, but if I had to sit, I'd pee all over myself. Goodwin paused, then began to chant to himself. *I will not eat. I will not eat. I am not hungry. I am not hungry.*

With his arm aching, Goodwin momentarily forgot about his hunger. *At last, I think I'm winning. If I get past supper time, I'll wait until Kohora brings the ham sandwiches.*

Goodwin swung his aching arm in a half circle, scratched it, pumped it up and down as if he were trying to hit the ceiling and finally put a choke hold on it. Spasms set in.

Small undulations at first, but gradually increased until the arm tried to do a curl by itself.

The battle between Goodwin and his arm continued. Goodwin tried to keep the arm extended, but he was forced to let it bend slightly. The more Goodwin struggled, the greater the pain, but when he didn't resist, the intensity of the pain decreased. Sweat poured from Goodwin. His mouth became dry, and his energy level dropped. An hour went by, and the exhausted Goodwin fell across the bed and went to sleep.

***

A loud voice erupted from Dr. Midwiff's office. "All of you old doctors are alike,"

Dr. Wells said, glaring at his coworker and pointing his finger at Dr. Midwiff's face.

"You should have been a butcher."

"Close the door," Dr. Midwiff said. "If you are going to shout. The report on the side effects of interferon aren't safe either. It's a gamble any way you look at it, but you're still willing to risk Mr. Phost's life. You're nothing but an ambitious young fool. Mr. Phost is my patient, and I will have the final word on the matter."

"But Dr. Midwiff …" Dr. Wells said. "Look what this could do for us the hospital.

News like that could make us wealthy. I could put out my own medical journal. You could play poker and the horses until you got tired."

"So I gamble a little, but I've never gambled with any of my patients' lives. Suppose Mr. Phost wants the operation?"

"Let me talk to him. I'll convince him to let me use interferon, but I'll need your help."

"What if I go along with you? We have no way of knowing whether Mr. Phost will cooperate or that this interferon will work."

"We have to try it," the excited Dr. Wells exclaimed. "I won't get another chance like this. I can see the headlines. **Doctor saves patient's hand from mysterious virus."**

"Okay," Dr. Midwiff said, shaking his head in disgust. "We had better start the treatments as soon as possible. The virus is growing fast."

***

"Wake up Mr. Phost. Wake up." Shouted nurse Aida Spintz as she vigorously shook Goodwin. "It's lunchtime."

Without opening his eyes, Goodwin grabbed his left arm and squeezed it. He thought his hand was causing him to shake. When the shaking continued, Goodwin cracked his eyelids and took a peek. Aida's buzzard-like face materialized like a genie from a lamp.

"What do you want? I'm not giving anymore blood, and I don't need a shot."

"I brought your lunch," she said, rolling the food cart up to Goodwin's portable table.

Goodwin rubbed his sleepy eyes and sat up. "I don't want lunch." *I was doing all right until she woke me up.* Strong hunger pangs set in again. Goodwin salivated, but he was determined not to eat until he went home later that afternoon. "Take it away," he said.

Goodwin brushed the cart with his right hand, almost knocking the food to the floor.

"I'll leave it. You might change your mind."

"I won't," Goodwin said. "I'll take it back to the kitchen, but I will have some water."

"I'm here to do a job and I'm going to do it," she said. "You take this food back to the kitchen and I'll return and hand-feed you myself. I've handled your kind before."

Goodwin threw his right hand up in the air. *Why argue with that old buzzard? Let her leave the food. I don't have to eat it.* "Leave it," Goodwin said. "It'll be here when you come back. Somebody else could be enjoying it."

Aida had poured Goodwin a glass of water and was fluffing Goodwin's pillow, when Dr. Wells and Dr. Midwiff came into the room. "Good afternoon, Mr. Phost," Dr. Midwiff said. "And you, too, nurse Spintz. How's the patient?"

"He refused to eat," Aida said eying Goodwin as if he were a child and Dr. Midwiff were his father.

"Doc, you know I don't like this food if you can call it that," Goodwin said. "I've been eating too much, and I don't need the extra pounds. Slop like this will put it on me."

"You have to eat something," Dr. Midwiff said. "I insist."

"I'd rather have the IV. At least I can't taste it."

Dr. Midwiff was right," Dr. Wells said. "You eat to keep your strength up in case we have to operate."

"I won't be here that long," Goodwin said. "Another four or five hours and I'll be home, where I can get some real food. What time is it, Dr. Wells?"

"Twelve-thirty," Dr. Wells replied. "Are you going somewhere?"

"You don't need me anymore," Aida interrupted. "That food is probably cold. I could bring Mr. Phost another plate."

"Don't bother. You old buz…" Goodwin said, catching himself. "If I want anything, I'll ring." Goodwin closed his eyes and clinched his right fist. *I'm not going to feed this thing anymore. Damned pains again. What can I say? I've got to get them out of here.*

"Mr. Phost. Are you okay?" Dr. Midwiff asked. "What can I do?"

"If you and Dr. Wells would leave…," Goodwin said, forcing a pleasant look.

"Please give us a minute," Dr. Wells said. "We'd like to discuss a method of treatment for your hand."

"Like what?"

"Dr. Midwiff has considered surgery," Dr. Wells said, "but I don't agree. We want you to help us make the proper call."

"What was my other choice?"

"Interferon," Dr. Wells answered.

"That cancer-fighting stuff?" Goodwin asked. "Before I make a decision, I have a few questions I want answered. Like, do I have cancer? You said I didn't, but maybe you changed your mind." Goodwin put his finger to his lips and shushed Dr. Wells before he could interrupt. "I'm not done talking. Will you stick with me? Rub it on or give me a pill?

How long will it take? When can I leave this place?

"There's no cancer," Dr. Midwiff said. "Dr. Wells can answer your other questions."

"Goodwin, Dr. Wells said," you will be given shots…"

"Wait a minute, Wells. I've had enough shots. Can I take a pill?" Goodwin winced.

Hunger pangs again? Old pal. Whoever, whatever you are, you'll have to wait.

"Goodwin, don't look so worried. The length of the treatments will depend on how your hand responds to them. We'll give you your first injection later today and keep you overnight, then you can come in for the remainder of your treatments."

"You guys always find a way to keep me here one more night. This is it. If you and Dr. Midwiff would leave, I'd like to get some rest."

"I thought you wanted to start right away," Dr. Wells said. "The sooner the better."

"I do, but give me another hour and we can get started." Goodwin's lips twitched as if he wanted to say more, but the words didn't come out.

"Mr. Phost, are you okay?" Dr. Midwiff asked. "You look tired and tense."

Goodwin struggled with the pain that was taking control of his body. He had to keep the doctors from becoming aware of his pain. He held his breath. The pain eased up. The room was silent as Goodwin fought his demons. Again, he tried to speak, but his lips quivered even more, and not a sound was uttered. The look in Goodwin's eyes changed from pleading to contempt, and his lips finally broke their silence. "Get out! Get out!"

Goodwin said, grasping his left arm. "Get out! I told you I would cooperate." Goodwin fell on the bed and rolled to the floor, still clutching his left arm.

***

It was late Sunday afternoon when Goodwin became aware of his latest dilemma. He was strapped to his bed, and an IV had been put in his right arm. Through half-opened eyes, Goodwin saw Dr. Midwiff, Kohora, and Dr. Wells staring down at him.

The wide canvas straps were placed around his body at his shins, thighs, waist, and chest. His right arm was at his side. The left arm was stretched out at a right angle to his body where it seemed to have been trying to free itself. Goodwin's head was the only part of his body that he could move with any amount of freedom.

"Take this crap off me," Goodwin said squirming to free himself.

"Relax, Honey," Kohora said, carefully stroking Goodwin's forehead.

"Relax? How in hell can I relax?" Goodwin asked, wiggling his head from side to side, trying to avoid Kohora's hand. "You let them do this to me?"

"When I got here, it was already done," Kohora answered.

"Mr. Phost. Control your temper," Dr. Midwiff said. "When we came to your room, you were on the floor writhing in pain and babbling about food. We had to sedate you and strap you to the bed."

"I don't remember what happened, but I'm fine now. Release me and I'll leave."

"Have you forgotten?" Dr. Wells asked. "Your treatments start tonight."

Goodwin strained against the straps that held him. They stretched like rubber bands.

Kohora ran her hand through Goodwin's hair and kissed him softly on his cheek. She slowly continued toward Goodwin's lips. The tenseness left his body as he sank back into the bed.

"Get these straps off me," Goodwin demanded. "Is this a hospital or a nut house?"

"Dr. Midwiff, please, please let Goodwin go," Kohora said. "I'm here now. He'll behave himself."

"What about the interferon treatments?" Dr. Wells asked.

"Is that all you can think of?" Dr. Midwiff asked. "Allow Mr. Phost to relax and regain his composure."

"Have you had anything to eat today?" Kohora asked.

"No," Goodwin answered. "I'm not going to eat until I go home."

"Are you sure?" Kohora asked. "I could go home and get something tasty like a couple of those big ham sandwiches."

Goodwin salivated. "No!" He replied. "Have them take these straps off."

Dr. Wells shook his head. "The straps should not be removed, but Goodwin is your patient. If you want to, what can I say? I'm trying to look out for Goodwin's welfare.

Look at his hand. It has grown without Goodwin feeding it."

Everyone's eyes focused on Goodwin's swollen hand. Dr. Midwiff took a closer look.

"It is larger," Dr. Midwiff said, "but just a little." Dr. Midwiff gently rubbed the swollen hand. "Does this hurt?" Goodwin lied as he shook his head. "Is it sore?"

"No."

"Look at that!" Kohora and Dr. Wells said in unison.

"That bubble moved," Dr. Wells said. "It's responding to Dr. Midwiff's strokes like it's keeping time."

"Like it's breathing," an excited Kohora said.

Dr. Midwiff took out his stethoscope and placed it over the left side of Goodwin's chest and listened. He heard a thump, thump, thump, and thump. The bubble rose and fell a split second after each beat of the heart. Everyone except Goodwin watched Dr. Midwiff's communication with the bubble. It appeared to return Dr. Midwiff's attention.

When he stopped rubbing his hand, it stopped rising and falling. Dr. Midwiff squeezed the bubble.

"The skin is a lot tougher than it looks," Dr. Midwiff said. "I doubt if you could penetrate it with a needle. "I felt something like a core."

"Unnnn!" Goodwin grunted as he rose up as far as the straps would allow. "What does it mean?" Goodwin asked. "What haven't you told me?"

"My best guess is," Dr. Midwiff paused. "You exposed yourself to a parasite, and it's feeding on you... Well, not you personally, but the food you eat."

"How? When? Where?" Goodwin asked with alacrity.

Dr. Midwiff's voice was filled with curiosity. "Have you been out of the country lately, or have been hiking and wading in some stream with an open sore?"

"No. No. And no," Goodwin replied. "What's that got to do with my hand!?"

"What does it mean, Goodwin?" Dr. Wells interrupted, "Something has entered your body via your mouth, nose, ears, or an open wound. We might have let it get the jump on us."

"What are you going to do about it?" Goodwin asked. "Can you cut it out?"

"An operation might endanger your life," Dr. Midwiff answered. "We'll have to let it run its course…like a pimple. When it comes to a head, then maybe we can operate."

"This is my last night in this place," Goodwin announced. "If it takes an ambulance to get me home."

"If you do," Dr. Wells said, "a hearse will bring you back for the autopsy. If I were in charge, you wouldn't be allowed to leave."

"Dr. Midwiff, you had better have Goodwin's IV bottle replaced," Kohora said. "This one is almost empty."

Dr. Midwiff picked up Goodwin's chart. "Mr. Phost, you've had three bottles since this morning. What are you doing?"

"Goodwin probably removed the tube and drank it." Dr. Wells said, laughing.

Dr. Midwiff shook his head. "Dr. Wells, that's not very nice. Who set the rate of flow? It's too fast." Dr. Midwiff looked at the restrained Goodwin.

"I take the blame," Goodwin said, "I was having spasms because I refused to eat, so I had the nurse put the IV in, but it was too slow, and the spasms got worse. I asked her to increase the flow, and that worked. ARE-THESE-STRAPS-COMING-OFF?" Goodwin strained and tugged with renewed strength. The bed rattled, and Goodwin continued his tantrum. Then abruptly, Goodwin stopped yelling and struggling.

"He passed out," Dr. Midwiff said with a sigh of relief. "With your permission, we'd like to give your husband his first shot of interferon. This would be a good time to do it."

"Can you remove the straps?" Kohora asked. "He's harmless now."

"I suppose it would be all right," Dr. Midwiff said.

"I don't," Dr. Wells said, moving toward the strapped Goodwin. "Let the straps stay."

"I'll decide whether or not the straps come off," Dr. Midwiff said. "I think I'm still in charge. Dr. Wells, you're here to help me. That's all. Do you understand?"

"That might be true," Dr. Wells said, "but I'm the expert here – genetic engineering, DNA and other related disciplines. You need me. I don't need you."

"But, I think your desire to be a part of this project is greater than my need for you,"

Dr. Midwiff said, "If you are beginning to feel indispensable, don't."

"Doctors," Kohora said. "Will you please stop arguing and do whatever is necessary to help my husband. He could be dying. Are the straps coming off?"

"Dr. Wells, get the interferon," Dr. Midwiff said, "I'll remove the straps." Dr. Wells left in a huff.

***

Thirty minutes later, Dr. Wells returned with the interferon. Goodwin had come to.

"I'm fine," Goodwin said. "I didn't like those straps. Thanks. You understand?"

"Yes, Mr. Phost," Dr. Midwiff answered. "Are you ready for your first injection?"

"That's a big needle, doc. Are you sure this is the only way?"

"We could always amputate," Dr. Wells said with a smirk. "You wouldn't want that."

"Shut up and give me the shot," Goodwin said. "No, Dr. Midwiff, you do it."

An angry Dr. Wells shoved the needle at Dr. Midwiff, almost sticking him in the hand.

"It doesn't matter to me who gives you the injection. When you recover, don't forget who saved your life. That doctor of yours wanted to amputate."

With a needle in hand, Dr. Midwiff slowly approached Goodwin. When he was inches from Goodwin's swollen hand, there was a rapid movement of the arm; a shaking like it was shivering. Dr. Midwiff reached out to grab it, but the hand jerked away and curled up toward Goodwin's bicep.

"Whoa there," Dr. Midwiff said. "This will only take a second. Relax."

"I can't doc... Uh," Goodwin said. "I mean, I'm not doing anything."

"You aren't?" Dr. Midwiff asked, renewing his effort to grasp Goodwin's flailing arm.

"I hurt all over," the sweat-drenched Goodwin said. "My arm is killing me."

"Relax!" Dr. Midwiff said. "It'll be over in a minute."

"I can't," Goodwin exclaimed as he tried to stop shaking.

"Maybe he's having an epileptic seizure," Dr. Wells said, moving quickly to assist Dr. Midwiff. "You should have left the straps on him. Next time, you'll listen to me."

Kohora steadied the IV as Dr. Wells held the weakened Goodwin's arm while Dr. Midwiff injected the interferon into his left upper arm.

Suddenly, Goodwin stopped shaking. "It's over, Mr. Phost," Dr. Midwiff said. "That wasn't so bad was it?"

Goodwin was silent. His eyes were closed, and he was pale.

"Honey, Honey," Kohora said. She vigorously shook Goodwin. "Are you okay?"

Goodwin remained silent, but he listened.

"Does Mr. Phost look dangerous?" Dr. Midwiff asked Dr. Wells.

"No, maybe I was wrong," Dr. Wells replied, "but I wouldn't trust him. He shouldn't be left alone."

"What are you suggesting? Kohora asked. "A guard?"

"No," Dr. Wells answered. "A male nurse."

"If anyone stays with my husband, it'll be me."

Through a maze of emotions, Goodwin's mind wandered. *I should have something to say about this. I'm the one suffering. Paining all over. I don't remember when Midwiff stuck me. I wanted to yell. I wanted to be left alone. Another minute and I would have asked for a pain killer to hell with machoism.*

Carefully shaking Goodwin, Kohora asked. "Are you…"

"I'm alive," Goodwin broke in. "If that's what you mean? I'M ALIVE!"

***

Monday morning came and Drs. Midwiff and Wells were in Goodwin's room looking at his chart.

"I don't believe it," a shocked Dr. Midwiff said. "I refuse to believe it. Nine bottles, nine bottles, nine bottles, nine IV bottles."

"What are you grumbling about?" Dr. Wells asked. "Let me see Goodwin's chart."

Dr. Midwiff handed Dr. Wells the chart. He looked at it. "Incompetence pure incompetence. Who was on duty last night?"

"Incompetent am I?" a haggard, sleepy-eyed Kohora asked. "I made sure the bottles were replaced as soon as they were empty."

"I . . . didn't mean it like that," Dr. Wells said.

At one point I fell asleep," Kohora said. "The nurse forgot and Goodwin suffered with hunger pangs. I had to hurry and get a full bottle myself. The chart is correct."

The two doctors looked at each other. "He needs to eat," Dr. Midwiff said. He walked over and examined Goodwin.

"Am I going to live?" Goodwin asked.

"Not unless you eat," Dr. Midwiff answered. "Why won't you eat?"

"Because whatever is feeding off me enjoyed the food more than I did. I get what's left and it has continued to grow. I tried to starve it, but I'm so hungry and weak. I didn't know I would get that hungry."

"Let me take a peep at your hand," Dr. Midwiff said, pulling the sheet back to expose Goodwin's hand. Speechless at first, Dr. Midwiff shook his head. "I don't believe it." He motioned for Dr. Wells and Kohora to witness what he saw. They approached the bed to take a look. Both of them stared without saying a word.

The silence caused Goodwin to open his eyes. He focused on their gaze. Goodwin raised his left hand up to take a look. "You . . .," Goodwin said as he reached out with his right hand and attempted to grab Dr. Wells; toppling the IV stand. The bubble on Goodwin's hand had doubled in size. It completely engulfed the space between his thumb and index finger. "You smart-alecked fool." Goodwin weakly pointed his finger at Dr. Wells. "What have you done to my hand? It's heavier than it was."

"Mr. Phost," Dr. Midwiff said. "Dr. Wells had the best of intentions. Would you object to your hand being weighed?"

"Weighed for what? He shot me up with whatever it was and look what happened. I had stopped feeding it and this manic fed it."

"Mr. Phost. Nobody's to blame," Dr. Midwiff said. "I'd still like to weigh your hand."

"You don't have to weigh it to see how it has swelled up or grown," Goodwin said.

"It's getting heavier all the time. Ask me and I'll tell you if it's bigger."

Dr. Midwiff shook his head. "Maybe it's that special formula we put in your IV. A bottle every hour. Maybe your virus thrives on it. A scale would be more accurate. We could match your food intake with the increase in the weight of your hand. We need to use every tool that's available to us. It won't hurt."

Goodwin looked at his fat hand. Still skeptical, Goodwin asked, "Will this help me leave this place sooner?"

"Of course, Mr. Phost," Dr. Midwiff answered. "The more you cooperate, the sooner you can leave provided it's safe to do so."

"You sounded sincere at first," Goodwin said, "but I'm not sure I can trust you."

Dr. Midwiff repeated, "If your life isn't in danger, you have my word."

"Bring on the scales," a jubilant Goodwin said. "I'm all for anything that will get me out of this place."

"I'll have the scales brought in," Dr. Midwiff said.

"Dr. Midwiff," Kohora interrupted. "Meanwhile, what if Goodwin's formula were changed? Kohora asked with a renewed sense of hope. "A less nutritious formula. Don't you see? Maybe you could figure out what it doesn't like. We could starve it."

Perturbed, Dr. Midwiff asked, "Mrs. Phost, what about your husband? We don't know what that thing is. Until we do, we'll treat it like any other infection with the latest drugs we have. We don't know if it's it or a new kind of infection. We don't know."

"Can you poison it?" Goodwin asked.

"Not without killing you." Dr. Wells answered, "And we don't want to do that."

With a last breath-like sigh, "You'd like that," Goodwin said. "Then you could really go after my wife."

A pinkish color spread over Dr. Wells' face. "I want you to come out of this as much as anyone." Dr. Wells said, his eyes flashing with embarrassment. It would be a big step for us and interferon. I can see it now in all of the most prestigious medical journals."

"Enough of this small talk," Dr. Midwiff said. "Let's get Goodwin's hand weighed.

The interferon could have caused his thumb to grow or swell like it did.”

“Could we step outside for a moment?” Dr. Wells asked Dr. Midwiff, beckoning.

***

Outside Goodwin's room, “You want me to be wrong.” Dr. Wells said. “You old doctors are behind the times. If you can't cut it out or penicillin it to death, you're lost.

You don't want to go back to school.”

“Have you finished?” An angry Dr. Midwiff asked.

“Not quite,” Dr. Wells replied. “Like my teachers in medical school, they went over the same stuff year after year. Do you think I'd be here if I were just another doctor with the same old hum-drum ideas?”

“You're talented,” Dr. Midwiff said, “but we could lose our jobs.”

“We haven't done anything out of the ordinary. If it gets out, we haven't done anything to be ashamed of, but it won't get out.”

“How are we going to prevent it?” Dr. Midwiff asked.

“Wait until something does happen, then we'll deal with it.”

“What if Mr. Phost dies?”

Dr. Wells laughed. “He's not going to die. Whoever heard of someone dying from a swollen thumb? Goodwin is young and strong, and he doesn't want to die.”

“What if the bubble gets larger?” Dr. Midwiff asked.

“We'll let it run its course, then do whatever has to be done.”

“Let's go back to Goodwin's room before he becomes suspicious and tries to leave.”

***

They returned to Goodwin's room, where his fat hand had been weighed and measured from the base of his palm to the tip of the bubble.

"How much did it weigh?" Dr. Midwiff asked Nicia Ling.

"Eleven pounds," she replied.

The two doctors looked at each other and then at Goodwin.

"That's rather heavy," Dr. Midwiff said. "Mr. Phost will need a sling before he goes home. He could probably use one now. I'll have one brought in."

"What's next?" Goodwin asked. "I want to go home."

"Goodwin Honey, you're going to have to eat something," Kohora said. She was seated close to the bed. Goodwin's swollen hand rested in her lap.

"Goodwin, she's right," Dr. Wells said, trying to sound really concerned.

Goodwin rubbed his stomach. *I'm so hungry. I could eat anything they put in front of me, but I can't eat. What! Those pains again.* Goodwin opened his eyes. "The IV is empty again," Goodwin said, motioning with his head.

"Mr. Phost, you'll have to eat," Dr. Midwiff said, "that's the last bottle. From now on you eat."

"My hand already weighs eleven pounds, and you want me to feed it. I won't."

"Mr. Phost," Dr. Midwiff paused and gathered his thoughts. "If you cooperate with us, the sooner you'll be able to leave. It's up to you."

"Honey, please eat just a little something," Kohora pleaded.

Goodwin shook his head. He gritted his teeth as the hunger pangs became more intense. A voice inside Goodwin's head repeated the following: eat, eat, eat. Every beat of his heart seemed to tap out the word: e-a-t, e-a-t, e-a-t, E-A-T!

"We can't let Goodwin dictate to us," Dr. Midwiff said. "Mrs. Phost, please remove the IV. I want him to eat."

"Just one more bottle," Kohora said as she moved to disconnect the IV. "Please."

"The pain-racked Goodwin spoke, "Okay, okay, I'll eat if eating will get me out of here sooner. No more shots. When do I leave?"

"When your hand goes down. Not until," Dr. Wells answered. "Not until."

"How far down?" Goodwin asked. "I'm leaving anyway."

"At least this far," Dr. Midwiff answered. He traced a pattern around Goodwin's right hand."

"You've got to be kidding," Goodwin said. "My hand will never be normal again."

"That's another reason why we weighed your hand," Dr. Midwiff said. "Weighing it is more accurate than looking at it and guessing."

Frustrated, Goodwin asked. "Are you going to operate? Will I leave this place alive?

What's wrong with me, doc?"

CHAPTER 8

It was six o'clock Tuesday morning, and Goodwin was still in the hospital. His hand hadn't returned to normal. Goodwin proudly wore his sling. The fat hand was still wrapped, but he didn't have to try and hide it. Goodwin tried to relax. He sat in one of the chairs in his room and read a magazine that Kohora had brought him. He heard a voice. At first, Goodwin thought the voice came from outside his room. Goodwin waited for the owner of the voice to enter his room. The voice grew louder, but nobody came through the door. Goodwin began to move his lips in unison with the phantom voice.

Goodwin realized he was mumbling aloud. He tried to stop the monologue, but it continued, although his lips had stopped moving. The harder Goodwin tried to stop, the louder the mumbling became from his lips and in his mind. The mumbling never stopped and the craving for food continued. Bacon and eggs plus a large slice of chocolate cake.

Goodwin tried to ignore his cravings, but they wouldn't go away. The voice returned.

"Order, order, order the food." Frustrated, Goodwin threw the magazine to the floor and rang for the nurse.

When the nurse entered the room, she asked, "Mr. Phost. What do you want this time?

I can't hear you. Stop mumbling and tell me what's wrong."

Goodwin had forgotten that he had rung for the nurse. Startled by the intrusion, "Get out," Goodwin said. "Get out now." The nurse left. Goodwin adjusted the sling that held his swollen hand. He looked at it and began to talk to it. He stroked it and the misshapen hand began to vibrate. The voice came back and began to whisper in Goodwin's mind.

"Beware, beware, BEWARE!" It said. Goodwin thought. *Beware of what?* He formed his lips to shape his words as though they were molded to fit into a box.

"Calm yourself."

"I am calm," Goodwin said, "I want to go home." *What am I saying?* Goodwin asked himself. *Am I losing it talking to my hand? I should let them cut you off.* In answer to Goodwin's threat, the hand bobbed up and down like a dribbled basketball. "I'll fix you,"

Goodwin mumbled. He removed it from the sling and pounded the hand against his thigh.

The hand swayed from side to side as if to avoid being smashed against Goodwin's leg.

Goodwin grabbed his wrist just below the hand and put a choke hold on it.

The voice returned. It seemed to say, *"Don't hurt me and I won't hurt you."*

Goodwin's lips moved. "I won't hurt you I'd break your neck if you had one." The hand bulged in and out like a puff adder. Goodwin grimaced as the back of his neck ached to the pulsations of the hand. Goodwin released his wrist and massaged his neck hoping the pain would go away.

Dammit Goodwin! What's wrong with you? He asked himself. *Nothing.* Goodwin answered. *Are you okay? I'm fine.* Back to reality: Goodwin regained his senses. Put his hand back in the sling. *Why is it so hot?* Sweat popped from his forehead. *Why don't they turn the air on?* With his left hand cradled in the sling, Goodwin walked over to the thermostat on the wall. *Sixty-nine? That's not low enough.* Goodwin wiped his brow and turned the thermostat down to sixty-two. Goodwin returned to his chair. He reached inside the sling and began to massage his injured hand. *I'm not getting any better. The pain in my arm has gotten worse. I can hardly breathe. What's happening to me?*

"Remove the sling," a little voice in Goodwin's mind said, "remove the sling," I said,

"Remove the sling, REMOVE-THE-SLING!" Without a thought, Goodwin removed his fat hand from the sling. *What a relief. I can breathe again.* He thought. His left hand slid off his lap. When Goodwin tried to retrieve it, without warning, the arm contracted and it was on Goodwin's left shoulder. It moved up and down as if it were trying to scratch an itch. Goodwin grabbed the swollen hand and pulled it away from his shoulder.

"Let me go. Let me go. Let me go," the phantom voice within Goodwin's mind said.

"I won't let you go," Goodwin said. "Behave yourself." Embarrassed, Goodwin looked around the room and hoped nobody had heard him. The left arm flailed at Goodwin's shoulder with such force, Goodwin reeled backwards in the chair. "Release me. NOW!"

The dialogue continued. "Why should I?" Goodwin asked the voice that resided in his mind. "You're a pain in the butt."

"Dare; beware. Release me, and the pain will stop."

I must be mighty hungry. Goodwin thought. *Talking to myself.* He summoned the nurse again.

"Mr. Goodwin, what can I do for you this time?" The nurse asked.

"Where's Kohora? She's my wife and a nurse, too."

"I don't know, but my name is Maze. I'm new here. I read your chart, and I must say yours is a strange case. How may I help you? Don't look so downhearted. I'm well qualified." Her voice, beauty, and temperament put Goodwin at ease.

"Maybe you're what I need. Someone with a fresh outlook." Goodwin told her why he had called for a nurse.

"Hand it, I mean, may I examine your hand? My, my, it looks like you hit it with a large hammer," nurse Maze said. She took the swollen hand and caressed it.

"Aaah," Goodwin crooned. He closed his eyes.

"Mr. Phost, are you alright? You're as red as a beet."

Goodwin smiled.

"I thought you needed help," nurse Maze said.

"I do Goodwin answered, "but for now, keep on doing what you're doing." Goodwin stretched his right arm toward the ceiling. "You could do this all night."

"Mr. Phost, I'm here to make sure your health problems are taken care of for which I'm well qualified. I'm not your personal masseuse."

"I won't apologize," Goodwin said. "You know what buttons to push."

Ignoring Goodwin's last remark. "What kind of medication are you on?" She asked.

"I'm not. They looked at it, poked it, and fed me that is, until I stopped eating. Do you have any suggestions?"

"Of course not. I've seen a lot of infections, but this is the first in 3-D. Most of them can be seen with the naked eye or under a microscope. I have never been able to pick one up." Nurse Maze continued to fondle Goodwin's swollen hand.

"Aaah, ooh," Goodwin moaned. "Pull up a chair. You could be here all night."

***

"Not if I can help it," a jealous Kohora said, bursting through the door with a tray of food. "You haven't eaten any solid food in a while. Have you lost your appetite or your mind?" Kohora stared at Goodwin and waited for an answer. Nurse Maze quickly released Goodwin's hand.

"Ow." Goodwin screamed as a sharp pain crawled from his infected hand to his arm.

Goodwin tried to ease the pain. "Hello, Honey. Nurse Maze was trying to massage some of the pain away, but you're here now. Want to take over?"

Kohora set the tray on the table. "No. I'll come back later," she answered. Kohora turned to leave.

"Wait," Goodwin pleaded. "I want you to stay. Talk to me. Feed me, please." Sweat popped from Goodwin's forehead as he grabbed Nurse Maze's arm. She stroked Goodwin's swollen hand. The pain became worse. Goodwin held Nurse Maze's arm tighter. Kohora rushed over to help Nurse Maze.

"Let her go," Kohora said.

"I'm trying," Goodwin said with a pained expression on his face. "If you come over here I'll let her go." Using his right hand, Goodwin jerked Kohora to him. The pain in the swollen hand returned, bringing with it one great spasm. The uncontrolled reaction knocked Nurse Maze's hand away and caused Goodwin to push Kohora away.

"Mr. Phost/Goodwin, what's wrong?" Nurse Maze and Kohora asked at the same time. Both of them struggled to maintain their balance.

"Get Dr. Midwiff," Kohora shouted. "Hurry."

The swollen hand twitched, and there was a whip-like motion with Goodwin at the end of the snap. When Dr. Midwiff arrived, the twitching had stopped.

Goodwin smiled. "Hello, doc. No more pain," he said, "but I'm very hungry."

Dr. Midwiff asked, "Do you still need me?"

"Don't look so frustrated, doc," Goodwin said, shaking his head.

"Are you sure?" Dr. Midwiff asked.

"What did I say?"

Dr. Midwiff looked at Goodwin's swollen hand. He gave Goodwin a pat on his shoulder and reluctantly left.

"Let me help you," Kohora said as she propped Goodwin upright. "I thought you had lost your appetite. You haven't eaten in a while."

"I know," Goodwin said, "but my arm and hand ached so badly, I forgot about food, but with the pain gone, greedy Goodwin is back." Goodwin devoured the two sandwiches Kohora had brought. "Is that all?"

"All that I brought, but I can get more from the dining hall. Wait here." Kohora had to laugh at what she said. "I'll be right back."

***

"And, what can I do for you this time, Mrs. Phost?" The man behind the food counter asked. "That eating machine you call a husband must be hungry again. The truth is I really missed fixing a plate for him when they took him off food."

"Two more sandwiches should be enough," Kohora answered. "Josh, I know you've heard that old saying, 'feed a cold...'"

"But Mrs. Phost," Josh interrupted, "That's not a cold your husband has."

"It's worse than a cold. We've been feeding it for the last three weeks. It must be some kind of tapeworm."

"Okay, Mrs. Phost, I'll fix Mr. Phost two deluxe club specials."

While waiting for Josh to fix Goodwin's sandwiches, Dr. Midwiff and Dr. Wells entered the cafeteria.

"Hi, Kohora," Dr. Wells said. "You have quite an appetite or are you here for your greedy husband?"

"My husband is not greedy, but since his illness, his appetite has doubled."

"Goodwin could be bulimic," Dr. Wells said. "Have you seen him eat and visit the bathroom?"

"When Goodwin visits the bathroom, I'm sure it's for natural causes."

"Tell lover boy we have more tests to run," Dr. Wells reminded Kohora. "We'll be over in about an hour. I hope there won't be any problems. I don't want to sedate or tie him down."

"Goodwin would never allow that," Kohora said, "you'd have to knock him out before he would let you sedate him…"

"There are ways…"

"That's enough," Dr. Midwiff interrupted. "I'm sure Mr. Phost wouldn't give us a hard time not deliberately anyway."

***

"Thanks, Honey," Goodwin said as he reached for the bag that Kohora had in her hand.

"What took so long? I thought about going to the cafeteria myself."

"I wasn't gone that long. Besides, you had two sandwiches a few minutes ago. Are you really that hungry?"

"I feel better when I eat," Goodwin replied.

Goodwin didn't seem to mind that the towel had slipped off his swollen hand. It was about the size of a honeydew watermelon.

"I know where all that food is going," Kohora said, "straight to your fat hand. I wish they could operate."

"I do too," Goodwin said, "but every time the doctors press and poke my hand, I pay for it. The pain is unbearable, or I pass out. I'd feel better if they could drain it or cut it off or something."

"Dr. Midwiff and Dr. Wells told me to tell you they would be over in a little bit. They have some more tests to run. The new tests should help them to determine if and when they would be able to operate."

"Are they going to take my hand off?" Goodwin asked. "Or will they let the air out of this bubble or whatever it is?"

"Who knows?" Kohora answered. "May I touch it?"

"I don't know," Goodwin replied.

"I won't poke or squeeze it," she said. "I'll rub it gently. You probably won't feel it."

"All I feel is pain," Goodwin said. He cupped the end of the bubble with his good hand as though he were trying to prevent it from rolling off the tray. "Maybe you should sit on my lap." Goodwin grabbed his wife and pulled her to his knee.

The left hand thrashed about dribbling itself. Throbbing pain penetrated Goodwin's body. It began in his left arm and ended in his head, alternating between the two points.

Goodwin released Kohora. She jumped to her feet and began to caress her husband's swollen hand.

"Whew," Goodwin sighed, "you know what to do. The pain isn't so bad anymore. Sit on my knee again."

Kohora shook her head. "That's not a good idea," she said. "You seem to be allergic to me. Don't look at me like that. Well, maybe not allergic, but something is wrong."

The frown on Goodwin's face faded. "You do have an effect on me, but I wouldn't call it an allergy," Goodwin said. "I want to be close to you."

"Don't look so sad. I won't sit on your lap, but I will caress your hand."

"How can you look at it?" Goodwin asked. "Let alone touch it?"

"You're my husband, and I love you," she answered.

As Kohora caressed Goodwin's ballooned hand, calmness engulfed his entire body.

Goodwin closed his eyes and was almost asleep when Dr. Midwiff and Dr. Wells came into his room. They were followed by two huge male nurses.

***

"What's going on?" Dr. Wells asked. "I thought we ran a hospital. Not a nursing home for big babies."

Goodwin opened his eyes a peep at a time. "So, it's you again," he said. "I thought you had gone home, but this is your home."

"We have other tests to run," Dr. Midwiff interrupted.

"I'm not taking anymore tests unless I can leave when you finish."

"You can leave anytime you want," Dr. Wells said. "Go ahead. Leave! Nobody will stop you. Leave!"

"Don't be foolish, darling," Kohora said. "That's not true. Is it Dr. Midwiff?"

"No, it isn't," Dr. Midwiff angrily replied. "Mr. Phost isn't in any condition to leave.

Look at his hand. He can't drive. Every time he tries to leave, the hand stops him. Until he stops passing out, Mr. Phost will remain here under our care."

"I'm not taking any more tests," Goodwin repeated. "I'd like to spend some time with my wife. Maybe she can help me decide. Otherwise, I'm okay."

"I'll bet you are," Dr. Wells said. "If I had a beautiful nurse, which happened to be my wife to caress my whatever, I'd get well soon, but I wouldn't be in any hurry to leave."

"Get this fool out of here before I bust this bubble on his head," Goodwin said. "I don't want him near me."

"I'm your only hope," a smug Dr. Wells said. "My genetic engineering background might make it possible for me to solve the problem with your hand."

"So far, all you've done is poke fun and poke my arm. I'm tired of both."

"Dr. Wells, Mr. Phost, control yourselves," Dr. Midwiff said. "What we need is peace and cooperation. This virus or whatever it is, has gotten out of hand pardon the pun."

"Calm down, honey," Kohora said while she caressed Goodwin's swollen hand. "Don't let Dr. Wells get to you. You'll need your strength to survive the operation."

"What operation!? Goodwin asked. "Nobody said anything to me about an operation."

"Sooner or later, Mr. Phost," Dr. Midwiff said. "We will have to operate or amputate.

It's inevitable. Unless you want to walk around like this for the rest of your life."

"It is the rest of my life," Goodwin said. "How long have I been in this place?"

"Going on three weeks," Dr. Midwiff answered. "I never thought it would be this long.

It's the strangest case I've ever seen. The virus or whatever it is, doesn't seem to be life threatening or contagious, but amputation might be the only cure."

"Maybe you could drain it," Goodwin said. "It might be a large pimple."

"I wish it were that simple," Dr. Midwiff said, "but it isn't a pimple. It would have come to a head by now. Mr. Phost, this is serious. Very serious."

"Life-threatening?" Kohora asked.

"It could be,"Dr. Wells answered. "It could be."

"But Dr. Midwiff said it wasn't," Kohora reminded Dr. Wells. "Who shall I believe?"

"Okay... So it might not be that serious," Dr. Wells said, "but we don't know how much larger it's going to get."

"If it gets any larger, my husband will need a pushcart to carry it in."

"I'd cut it off myself," Goodwin said, grimacing as a sharp pain traveled from his swollen hand up to his left shoulder. "I didn't mean it," Goodwin mumbled.

"Didn't mean what?" Kohora asked. "Who are you talking to?"

"Myself I guess," Goodwin replied. "I felt some pain."

"Let's get on with the tests," Dr. Wells said. "I have other tests to analyze."

"Come on, Wells," Goodwin said. "You've spent most of your time in the lab trying to figure out what's wrong with me."

"That's why I want to take more tissue and blood samples. It's probably something you ate."

"No time for jokes," Goodwin said. "It's my life you're talking about."

"I was only kidding."

"Wells, we don't kid. I don't like you. Never have."

"Why?"

"You know why," Goodwin answered, looking at Kohora.

"There's nothing to be jealous about," Dr. Wells said. "We're coworkers. That's it."

"Let's stick to the business at hand," Dr. Midwiff said. "We must run more tests."

"Here's the wheelchair," the nurse said, pushing the door open.

"Wheelchair?" Goodwin asked. "I can walk."

"Just a precaution," Dr. Wells said. "We don't want you to become fatigued."

"There's nothing wrong with my legs."

"Mr. Phost. Make it easy on yourself," Dr. Midwiff said. "Use the wheelchair."

"I'm not a wheelchair person," Goodwin said, flexing his right arm.

***

Dr. Wells rang the nurse's station. In a couple of minutes, two huge male nurses came into Goodwin's room.

"They look like teddy bears to me," Goodwin said. "Look at those guts."

"You need us?" One of the nurses asked.

Dr. Wells looked at Goodwin. "We have an unwilling patient," Dr. Wells said. "He'll need some help getting into the wheelchair." The two nurses started toward Goodwin.

Goodwin stood up. He let his swollen hand drop to his side. Goodwin's eyes glared with defiance. "I won't use that chair, and nobody's going to make me."

The nurses stopped in their tracks.

"Don't stand there looking at him," Dr. Wells said. "Put him in the chair if you have to strap him in it."

One of the nurses reached for Goodwin. Zap! Went Goodwin's swollen hand against the nurses face. The blow sent the nurse sprawling into Dr. Wells. Goodwin pulled his hand back in pain. He was surprised at how light the hand felt. Goodwin looked at the other nurse.

"Come on and get yours," Goodwin said, slamming his right fist into the other nurse's face, knocking him into the wall.

"Stop, Honey," Kohora pleaded. "Please stop."

"Come on, boys," he said, beckoning with his right hand. "Have some more." Goodwin taunted. "Do you still think I need a wheelchair?"

"Call security," Dr. Wells said. "You can't treat our employees like that. You maniac. It's for your own good."

The nurses kept their eyes on Goodwin. "I thought the man was ill," one of them said.

"He doesn't seem to need the wheelchair."

"You're damned right. I don't need it," Goodwin said. "You'll have to take me out on a stretcher before you put me in that chair."

"You want to get tough," the other nurse said. "We'll show you what tough is."

The swollen hand struck first, followed by the right hand. Both nurses went their separate ways. They banged into whatever was in their path.

Kohora put her arms around Goodwin. "Please stop."

"Ah, that felt good," Goodwin said. "I feel so relaxed."

"Dr. Midwiff, stop them," Kohora said. "They might hurt my husband."

"I'll sue the bastard," one of the nurses said. "We don't get paid to take a beating. Dr. Wells, if you want him in the wheelchair, you'll have to put him in it yourself."

"Where is that darn security guard?" Dr. Wells asked.

"That won't be necessary," Goodwin said. "If you let me walk to the lab. What's the guard going to do? Shoot me?"

"Mr. Phost, nobody's going to shoot you," Dr. Midwiff said. "You may walk. I'm sorry you had to go through this. Sometimes Dr. Wells goes overboard."

"I'm going to the lab," Dr. Wells said. "Have Goodwin there in the next fifteen minutes. Come on, fellows."

"Why do you put up with him?" Goodwin asked. "You're in charge aren't you?"

"He's the best at what he does," Dr. Midwiff answered. "He might be your only hope."

"Honey, are you all right?" Kohora asked. "Did you hurt your hand?"

"My hand is fine," Goodwin answered. "I can't remember when I've enjoyed myself so much."

"Let's hope the nurses won't file charges against you or the hospital," Dr. Midwiff said. Shall we go to the lab?"

***

At the lab: "Macho man finally made it," Dr. Wells said.

"Watch your mouth, Wells," Goodwin said. "Dr. Midwiff convinced me that it was necessary. Otherwise, I wouldn't have come."

"Lie down over there on that table," Dr. Wells said.

"I'd rather sit. I feel more at ease."

"Are you going to sit if or when we operate?" Dr. Wells asked.

"I'll think about it," Goodwin answered.

"Okay, Goodwin," Dr. Wells said. "Sit on this stool and place your fat hand on the table. We won't get into any more hassles."

"Wells. What's that?" Goodwin asked.

"It's a sterilizing solution," Dr. Wells answered. He swabbed the area where he was going to draw some fluid from Goodwin's left arm. "You'll have to be still."

"I'm not moving," Goodwin said. "I can't help it if I'm a little nervous."

"Hold it steady. I can't put the needle in the right spot if you don't."

"I'm trying doc, but I can't stop shaking."

"Come on macho man. I know you can," Dr. Wells said.

"What's my name Wells?" Goodwin asked. "I'll not ask you again."

"Okay Goodwin," Dr. Wells said. "Hold your arm steady please."

"Back off Wells," Goodwin said. "Let me relax for a minute or two."

"We don't have a lot of time," Dr. Midwiff said. "The bubble has gotten larger."

"Maybe it'll burst by itself," Goodwin said, "then I wouldn't have to go through this no nonsense test."

"Goodwin, are you ready?" Dr. Wells asked. "I'm not going stand here and hold this needle all day."

"I'm hungry," Goodwin said. "I need some food before I can do anything. That's why I'm so nervous. Tell him Dr. Midwiff."

"I'm hungry too," Dr. Midwiff said. "Dr. Wells, are you coming? Kohora, will you help Goodwin back to his room? I'll have something sent to you and Goodwin."

"I'll go too and make my husband his favorite sandwich," Kohora said.

"We might as well do the test some other time," Dr. Wells said. "Goodwin, you'd do anything to stop me from doing my job. Okay, but we'll have to wait at least a couple of hours before we can draw the fluid from your arm."

"Dr. Wells, will you shut up. Please?" Dr. Midwiff said. "How would you feel if you had a bulbous extension the size of a small watermelon hanging off the end of your arm?"

"My only concern is for our patient," Dr. Wells said, "but I don't like his attitude. He could be more cooperative."

They left for the cafeteria.

CHAPTER 9

Back in Goodwin's room, "Here's two of your favorite double-decker sandwiches and a quart of milk to wash them down," Kohora proudly declared.

"I didn't want that, Dr. Wells, to know it, but my hand was aching and it still hurts," Goodwin said. "The hospital's cafeteria makes the best turkey and ham sandwiches in this world. I feel better now. The sandwiches should hold me for another hour or two."

"Shall I call the doctors?"

"No. Let's talk."

"Talk? No caressing or kissing?" Kohora asked. "You must be worried or sick."

"Look at it," Goodwin said, pointing to his fat hand. "It has grown right before our eyes, or haven't you noticed?"

Dr. Wells and Dr. Midwiff returned from the cafeteria.

"No, I hadn't noticed," Kohora replied.

"What do you think they'll find?" Goodwin asked. "I'm scared."

"Don't worry. We have the finest surgeons anywhere to be found."

"Shall we proceed with the test?" Dr. Wells asked, grinning.

"That was mighty quick," Goodwin said. "What did you do? Drink your lunch?"

"Mr. Phost, we have to draw some fluid from your left arm right away."

"Let's go. I'm ready," Goodwin said, trying to sound enthusiastic.

***

At the lab, Goodwin laid his injured hand on the table. He heard the voice again.

It seemed to say, **"Don't, don't, don't."**

The arm began to move from side to side as if someone were trying to roll it off the table. Goodwin grabbed the fleshy dome-shaped growth. He tried to stop it from flopping.

Goodwin's stomach cramped, and he felt as though he were going to vomit. Dr. Wells moved closer with the needle. "What the hell?" Dr. Wells asked, moving his head to one side as the hand made a swipe at it. "Goodwin, what are you trying to do to me? Anger flooded his voice.

"Dr. Wells! Move back," Dr. Midwiff said. "Let Mr. Phost calm down. Kohora, calm your husband."

"I'll calm down when everyone leaves me alone," Goodwin said. "I don't need a baby sitter. I told Wells not to poke me with that needle."

"That's the only way to get a sample of the fluid," Kohora said. "If there were another method, they would use it."

"Get that needle poking manic out of here," Goodwin said.

"Do you want to lie down?" Dr. Midwiff asked. "Does your arm hurt?"

"I ache all over," he answered, shaking his head.

"I want a sample today," Dr. Wells asserted. "Not tomorrow."

"If you want it, come and get it," Goodwin said, raising his right hand and shaking his fist at Dr. Wells.

"Dr. Wells! Back off!" Dr. Midwiff stepped between the two men. "Dr. Wells, Mr.Phost isn't going to let you do it today."

"Tomorrow, either," Goodwin mumbled.

"If this weren't such an important case," Dr. Wells said, "I'd walk out and forget about it. I'll be back."

"Dr. Wells...," Dr. Midwiff began.

"Let him go," Goodwin said. "Maybe things will calm down now."

"How are you, Mr. Phost? Do you want something to relax your nerves?"

"Can I take it by mouth?" Goodwin asked.

"Yes," Kohora answered.

"I was only kidding," Goodwin said. "I don't want the pill either. They might try to drug me and get the fluid anyway."

"Don't look so worried, Mr. Phost. May I examine the bubble?" Dr. Midwiff asked as he moved cautiously toward Goodwin's swollen hand. "I won't hurt you."

"Who are you talking to?" Goodwin asked. "Me or my hand?"

"Both of you I guess," Dr. Midwiff replied, touching the swollen hand as though he were looking for a leak.

"Go ahead, doc. It won't bite you," Goodwin said. "That doesn't hurt."

"Ah, this is most unusual. My, my Mr. Phost. I've never seen anything like this."

Dr. Midwiff said, scratching his chin. "Most unusual?"

"What do you think, doc? Are you going to let the water out?"

"If it can be drained safely," Dr. Midwiff answered. "Shall I call Dr. Wells?"

"No!" Goodwin answered, frowning.

"I find the growth quite intriguing," Dr. Midwiff said. "It looks delicate, but it is very, very firm."

"This waiting is getting to me," Goodwin said. "Maybe you can take the samples."

"Are you sure?"

"Yes."

"Kohora. Get the syringe," Dr. Midwiff said.

"Right away," she said, walking over to a table that had a tray that held the instruments Dr. Midwiff needed.

Dr. Midwiff resumed his examination of Goodwin's bulbous hand. Goodwin flinched.

"Am I pressing too hard?" Dr. Midwiff asked. "You had that look again."

"Here you are Dr. Midwiff," Kohora said holding the tray with the instruments on it so Dr. Midwiff could get what he needed.

Dr. Midwiff picked up a small syringe. "This will do just fine," he said.

"What can I do?" Kohora asked.

Dr. Midwiff smiled. "Keep your husband's mind on you." He moved the syringe toward the bulbous growth. Dr. Midwiff reached out with his left hand so he could guide the needle in. Clap! Dr. Midwiff was sent sprawling to the floor as the swollen hand popped like the end of a whip, unleashing a blow to Dr. Midwiff's face.

Goodwin turned cherry red. "I'm sorry, doc. Real sorry," he said.

"Let me help you up," an embarrassed Kohora said. "There's something terribly wrong with my husband."

"Yes, there is," Dr. Midwiff said as he tried to shake the blow off. "You leave me no choice Mr. Phost. You will have to be strapped down."

"Not without my consent," Goodwin said.

"Honey...," Kohora began.

"No! Better yet," Goodwin said, "not living."

***

Down at the hospital cafeteria, "Make sure Mrs. Phost uses everything from this section," Dr. Wells told the cook. "Do you understand?"

"Yes, Dr. Wells," the cook replied. "Whoever eats this will be out like a light."

"Remember, I'll take full responsibility."

***

Back at the lab, "I-am-hungry," Goodwin said. "Bring-me-some-food."

"Dr. Midwiff, are you okay?" Kohora asked as she examined his face.

Dr. Midwiff nodded.

Kohora smiled weakly. "I'll go to the cafeteria and make Goodwin a couple of his favorite sandwiches. Be right back."

"I'll go with you," Dr. Midwiff said. "Mr. Phost needs some time to himself. I could use a break, too. Stay here until we get back."

***

When they left, Goodwin went back to his room. Alone, Goodwin contemplated his next move. *I don't want to hurt anybody, but I hear these voices. Am I losing it? It should have been that weasel, Wells. It wouldn't have been a slap either. I would probably choke him.*

Goodwin's thoughts were interrupted by the return of the frantic Dr. Midwiff, Kohora and Dr. Wells.

***

"Why didn't you tell us you were going back to your room?" They asked in unison.

"A spur-of-the-moment thing," Goodwin replied.

"I hope you're in better spirits Mr. Phost," Dr. Midwiff said, holding the door open for Kohora, who carried Goodwin's sandwiches. She was followed by Dr. Wells.

"How's your face?" Goodwin asked. "I'm sorry for what happened."

"Except for a little soreness, I'm okay," Dr. Midwiff replied.

"Here's your food, darling," Kohora said. She used the bed's crank to help Goodwin sit up. He had opened one of the wrappers and had begun to gobble the sandwich before he was upright. "Easy, honey. It's not going anywhere. If I didn't know better, this was your first meal today."

"Goodwin is greedy," Dr. Well said. "Just plain greedy."

Goodwin ignored Dr. Wells' statement and continued to devour his sandwiches.

"It's good that you don't let Dr. Wells get under your skin," Kohora said

"Greed overrides everything," Dr. Wells said, "Even Goodwin's dislike for me."

"When you finish eating," Dr. Midwiff said, "we'll have to go back to the lab and strap you to the table."

"I've lost my appetite," Goodwin said, putting his sandwich down. "Nobody's going to strap me to anything. I'm not sick. Have you ever seen a sick man eat as much as I?"

"I haven't seen many well men eat as much as you," Dr. Wells said. "You must be feeding that hand, too."

"I'll fix you," Goodwin said, reaching for Dr. Wells. "I'm... and Goodwin collapsed.

"What's wrong, honey?" Kohora asked. She bent down over the bed and rubbed Goodwin's cheeks. "What have you done to my husband?"

"Don't look at me," Dr. Wells said with an air of innocence. "Goodwin is sick. Let's move him back to the lab and strap him down now."

"There will be no straps until Mr. Phost comes to," Dr. Midwiff said.

"Nobody is going to strap my husband down or do anything to him without my permission."

"Get the male nurses in here," Dr. Midwiff said. "I'll take a closer look at Goodwin."

"You rang for us, Dr. Midwiff?" One of the male nurses asked.

"Yes. Take Mr. Phost back to the lab."

"This guy is heavy," the other nurse said. "I'm glad we have gurneys."

Goodwin was strapped to the gurney and taken to the lab.

Kohora smiled. "That's one of the advantages of having male nurses."

"We're more than just strong backs. We went through the same training you had."

"Don't take offense, fellows," Kohora said. "Be careful."

As the nurses rolled Goodwin to the lab, "Slow down," Dr. Midwiff said.

"Why are you pampering that maniac?" Dr. Wells asked.

***

After being placed on the table, Goodwin woke up. "What are these men doing here?" He asked. "They didn't get enough from the last time? Where's my sandwich? I'm still hungry." Goodwin sat up and let his legs hang over the side of the table.

"Here's what's left," Kohora said. She gave Goodwin the bag, which contained one sandwich and what was left of the partially eaten one.

"We'll have to strap you down," Dr. Midwiff said, but I'll let you finish eating."

"When I finish this food, I'm leaving this place. Nobody's going to stop me."

Goodwin looked directly at the two male nurses.

"Wait," Dr. Wells said when one of the nurses started toward Goodwin. "Maybe we shouldn't put straps on Goodwin.

Surprised by Dr. Wells' decision not to have him strapped down, Goodwin continued to devour his snack, but he kept an eye on the two nurses. After he had finished eating

Goodwin felt faint. *Not again,* Goodwin thought. *I fed this thing.* He swung his legs back upon the table and stretched out. Goodwin let out a yawn. He mumbled a few words and passed out. His infected hand hung over the side of the table.

"Goodwin!" Kohora shouted. She went over and quickly raised Goodwin's fat hand up and placed it across his chest.

The male nurses watched.

Dr. Midwiff was there in a flash, too. He gave Goodwin a cursory inspection. "Don't just stand there," Dr. Midwiff said. "Get a gurney and take Mr. Phost back to his room.

Hurry! I might as well draw some fluid from Mr. Phost while he is out."

Angrily, Kohora asked, "Dr. Midwiff, don't you think you should be trying to find out why Goodwin passed out."

"Yes, but I need the fluid before he regains consciousness," Dr. Midwiff replied.

When Dr. Midwiff approached the swollen hand with the syringe, the hand tried to roll off Goodwin's chest in an effort to avoid the syringe.

"What's going on?" The surprised Kohora asked. Her training as a nurse kicked in. She reacted instantly and grabbed Goodwin's left arm just below the wrist. Without a conscious Goodwin to help the hand, Kohora easily held it down while Dr. Midwiff withdrew the fluid from it.

"Dr. Wells, will you take this sample to the lab? Please."

Without a word, Dr. Wells yanked the syringe from Dr. Midwiff and left. Still holding Goodwin's left wrist with the bubble throbbing up and down, Kohora asked in a subdued tone. "Where do we go from here?"

"I don't know," Dr. Midwiff answered. "I don't want to, but I have no other choice than to have Goodwin strapped down."

"Why?"

"Who knows what Goodwin will do when he learns that he'll have to stay in the hospital until his infected hand is amputated or the swelling goes down."

"You can't do that," an angry Kohora declared. "I won't let you. It wouldn't be legal."

"My mind is made up," Dr. Midwiff said.

Kohora continued. "On what grounds!?"

"Goodwin has an infection of some kind?" Dr. Midwiff asked. "Right?"

Kohora nodded. "But it's not contagious is it?" She asked.

"We don't know," Dr. Midwiff answered. "But to be on the safe side, Goodwin should remain here. As on what grounds? I'll put him in quarantine. Don't be angry. I'll arrange it so you can take care of him."

"I still don't like it," Kohora said, "but if I'm assigned as his nurse, I'd feel better."

CHAPTER 10

It was Wednesday the next day when Goodwin stirred. "Where am I?" the stunned Goodwin asked while struggling to free himself. Kohora sat in a chair beside the bed.

Goodwin's fat hand rested on her lap. "Kohora! What have they done to me? Answer me!" Goodwin continued his effort to free himself. Goodwin's swollen hand bounced up and down on his wife's lap. With his right hand, Goodwin pulled on the bed railing. He banged his fist against it.

"Mr. Phost," the ashen-faced Dr. Midwiff said. He hesitated. "I have some good and bad news. First, the bad news. "You'll have to remain here until we find out exactly what it is that you have contracted...," Dr. Midwiff paused, "or the bubble bursts, or we amputate it. From this day on, you will be moved to a more secluded and sterile room.

Your visitors will be limited to hospital staff who will wear the latest in germ deterrence attire. The good news: Kohora will be a part of that special task force. How does that sound?"

Bang, bang, bang went the red-faced Goodwin's right fist against the bed rail. *Don't let them do this!* The little voice in Goodwin's head interrupted. "I won't," Goodwin said aloud. "You can bet on it."

Dr. Midwiff looked at Kohora, who was shaking her head.

"Are you talking to us?" Dr. Midwiff asked.

Goodwin caught himself. "You bet I am," he replied. "I won't let you keep me here."

"Who's going to stop us?" Dr. Wells asked.

Ignoring Dr. Wells' question, Goodwin asked. "What about these straps? How will I take a crap? What about my fat hand? Will I be able to shower or shave?"

"One question at a time, Mr. Phost," Dr. Midwiff said. "Until you behave, you'll have to use a bedpan. Your wife will help you shower and shave. I'll have a tray brought in for your hand."

Goodwin was strapped to his bed. His legs were bound, but the straps on his upper body ran under his back and across his chest. His arms were left free. Goodwin's upper body could be raised whenever he wanted to eat or watch TV.

***

A week later, on a Wednesday morning around 10 a.m., Dr. Midwiff made his rounds to check on his patients. Because of his status, Goodwin was at the top of his list. When he entered Goodwin's room, bang went Goodwin's fist against the bed's railing.

"Somebody call the police," Goodwin shouted. "I'm being held against my will. I'll sue. Where's my wife? Somewhere with that Dr. Wells. Why isn't she in here with me?

I'll tear this bed apart."

"Mr. Phost," Dr. Midwiff said. "I'll have to sedate you if you don't calm down."

Goodwin paused for a moment. "Sedate me!" he shouted, raising the fat hand as high as he could. Goodwin continued. "Better yet, cut my arm off. Put a hole in that bubble."

"Mr. Phost!" Dr. Midwiff shouted back at Goodwin. "You're not the only one that's frustrated. You'll have to bear with us until a solution to your problem has been found."

"I want to go home. Solution or no solution. I need some exercise."

"Quarantined patients aren't allowed to walk the halls."

"But I'm not really a health risk and you know it."

"Maybe so," Dr. Widwiff said, "but you are a flight risk."

"Where could I go?" Goodwin asked. "Get my wife in here. She could walk with me."

"I'll have her paged, but I can't promise you anything," Dr. Midwiff said.

"Nurse Phost, please report to the quarantine area," boomed from the PA system.

***

"Has something wrong with my husband?" A worried Kohora asked Dr. Midwiff as she rushed into Goodwin's room.

"He's okay for now," Dr. Midwiff replied, "but I don't know how long it'll last. Goodwin has been most uncooperative."

"Goodwin, what have you done?" She asked, giving Goodwin a firm look. "If you want to get well, you'll have to behave yourself."

"I'm tired of this place," Goodwin said. "I want to go home. I want this overblown bubble or whatever it is, I want it cut off . . ."

May I examine your hand?" Dr. Midwiff reached for Goodwin's fat hand.

"If I let you touch my hand, what's in it for me?"

"I'm trying to be nice, Mr. Phost, but you're trying my patience. Either you let me see your hand voluntarily, or I will sedate you and do as I please."

"Calm down, dear." Kohora interrupted. "They're doing what they can to come up with a plan to get rid of it. You'll have to work with them."

"I'm trying." Goodwin paused.

"Mr. Phost have you finished? Dr. Midwiff asked.

"No!"

"You can finish while I examine your hand," Dr. Midwiff said, grabbing Goodwin's fat hand. The struggle was on. The doctor against the fat hand and Goodwin's right hand.

The little voice in Goodwin's head had its say. *That-a-boy, don't let'im do that to you.*

"I won't," Goodwin shouted aloud. "I won't."

Kohora gripped the bubble with both hands, but it was short-lived because of its mushiness. The fat hand bounced around, and she lost her grip.

"Who are you helping?" Goodwin asked Kohora. "I need you on my side."

"I'm not on anybody's side," Kohora declared. "I'm a nurse trying to do my job."

The struggle continued. With his right hand, Goodwin pulled one of the doctor's hands from the wrist of his fat hand. Dr. Midwiff lost his balance, and Goodwin pulled him across the bed railing and onto the bed. Kohora had tried to keep her grip, but it was more like she was kneading dough. The fat hand with the bubble bounced up and down and all around as it lashed out at the doctor.

Two male nurses were called. They subdued Goodwin and his wayward hand while Dr. Midwiff gave Goodwin a mild sedative. Goodwin slowly stopped struggling, but the hand continued to vibrate. It eventually fell victim to the sedative, too. Dr. Midwiff resumed his examination of the fat hand.

"I hope it's ready to come to a head," Dr. Midwiff said. "Then we might find out what we're dealing with. Until then, Mr. Phost will remain in the hospital."

Kohora shook her head. "Goodwin would be better off if he were at home," she said.

"I'd like that too," Dr. Midwiff said. "But he passes out every time he tries to leave the hospital. Deep down inside, Goodwin might not want to leave."

"Maybe if he were taken out in a wheelchair, it wouldn't be so bad," Kohora said.

"I'll think about it," Dr. Midwiff said. "On the other hand, I would be extremely worried. What if Goodwin wanted to take a walk?"

"It would be in the house or in the yard," Kohora answered. "He wouldn't go very far.

Goodwin would have to carry his swollen hand with him."

"Umm, that would present a problem," Dr. Midwiff said, scratching his head.

Like a child that had suddenly made a startling discovery, Kohora said. "Goodwin could use one of those papoose pouches that parents use to carry their babies in."

"That might work," the bemused Dr. Midwiff said. "Of course, Goodwin would have to agree. There would be other restrictions, too."

"Like what?"

"Suppose he became violent? What would you do? I know you're a nurse, but tell me how would you handle him?"

"The easiest way would be to sedate him," Kohora answered. "What's so funny?"

"You saw how hard it was for the four of us to sedate Goodwin, and he was strapped to the bed. We'll have to come up with some kind of emergency plan."

An eerie silence permeated the room as Kohora and Dr. Midwiff tried to devise a plan that might work. One that Goodwin would agree to.

"An around-the-clock male nurse might work," Dr. Midwiff said.

"Where would he sleep?" Kohora asked. "Our place is small."

"But you do have two bedrooms?"

"Yes, but Goodwin wouldn't like it."

"He doesn't have a choice," Dr. Midwiff said. Sternness punctuated every word. "If you think Goodwin will be better off at home, I'll see what I can do."

***

Two weeks went by while Dr. Midwiff worked on having Goodwin released to his wife, but it all seemed in vain.

"Easy fellows," Kohora said. She cautioned the two heavy-set male nurses to help Goodwin got out of bed.

"I'm not helpless," Goodwin said, jerking his right hand away from one of the nurses.

"Hold my left hand and don't drop it." Goodwin laughed.

The nurses walked Goodwin to the bathroom, where they closed the door.

This is one big mess. Goodwin thought. *I'm glad I'm wearing this gown. I can see myself now. Pulling my pajamas down. It's bad enough with this damn fat-ass hand in my lap.*

After Goodwin had taken care of business, he pulled the swollen hand tightly against his body. That didn't work, so Goodwin let it hang down when he stood up to wipe his butt. After he finished, Goodwin opened the door.

"Don't just stand there," Goodwin said, waving his right hand. "Take my fat hand and help me to my bed."

At the bed, Goodwin refused to lie down. Instead, he stood tall with the fat hand at his side. "No straps, boys," Goodwin said. "I mean it!"

The nurses closed in on Goodwin. Slap went his right hand upside one of the nurses' face. The fat hand took care of the other nurse with a blow to the groin. Kohora watched.

"Stop it," she yelled. "Goodwin, it's for your own good."

The two nurses regrouped for another attempt to put Goodwin back in the bed. Kohora stood between Goodwin and the nurses.

"Calm down," she said. "I'll have Dr. Midwiff paged."

Goodwin stood his ground. He held his fat hand at his waist with his good hand. The three men stared at one another. Before either side could launch an attack, Dr. Midwiff burst through the door.

"Mr. Phost, why aren't you in bed?" He asked. "I'm tired of your antics. Get back in the bed or I will have to sedate you. I've been trying to get the proper paperwork done so you could go home, and this is what I get for my effort."

The surprised Goodwin dropped his head. "I didn't want to be strapped down in that bed," he said. "And I won't be. You do whatever you think you have to." Goodwin raised his fat hand up with the help of his right hand. "I don't want to hurt anyone, but if you try to have me strapped to that bed, I won't be responsible for what might happen."

Kohora turned and faced Goodwin. "I understand your frustration, but you'll have to cooperate with Dr. Midwiff."

"When I go home," Goodwin said. "I won't be strapped to my bed. So! Why do I have to be strapped to this bed?"

"Because of your behavior," Dr. Midwiff answered.

"I could wait until I get home and act the same way."

Kohora shook her head. "If I thought you would pull a stunt like that," she said. "I wouldn't sign for your release . . . unless you want to go home in a straitjacket."

"You wouldn't," Goodwin said. "How could you?"

Kohora smiled. "You're right," she said, "You'd have to stay here."

"What's it going to be?" Dr. Midwiff asked, feeling a little more confident.

"I tell you what," Goodwin said. "Put me in a wheelchair and let my wife check me out now. Otherwise, we have a problem."

Dr. Midwiff took a deep breath. "I don't agree with your proposal, but I'm trying to be reasonable. Kohora what do you think?"

"It might work," she answered, "but there's something I need to discuss with you."

"What is it?"

"I'll need an emergency kit."

Somewhat puzzled by Kohora's request, Dr. Midwiff paused before he spoke.

Kohora squinted as though the sun were shining in her eyes. She motioned for Dr. Midwiff was to come over so she could tell him something.

Moving quickly, Dr. Midwiff approached Kohora and leaned close to her. Kohora's lips almost touched his ears. "Oh yes, the emergency kit," he said. He became aware that Kohora had a backup plan if this home trial didn't work.

She placed her hand on Dr. Midwiff's shoulder to steady him and whispered, "I'll need a fast-acting sedative and a straitjacket. Can you get those items for me?"

"Will do," Dr. Midwiff said, feeling relieved. "You think of everything."

"What was that about?" Goodwin asked while watching with anxiety.

There was complete silence. Goodwin cradled his fat hand against his stomach with the support of his right hand.

"Somebody better answer me!" Goodwin said, staring at the door.

"If you must know, I told Dr. Midwiff I'd need some pain killers and an IV," Kohora said. "If you are unable to eat. Are you satisfied?"

"Why all the hush-hush?" Goodwin asked, shaking his head.

"I didn't want to upset you," Kohora replied.

"Why would that upset me?" Goodwin asked.

"You'll have to answer that," Kohora bluntly answered. "You know yourself better than I do. If you still want to go home, drop it so we can get you ready."

Goodwin's disposition changed, and he sat on the side of the bed watching his wife and doctor. "No straps," Goodwin said. "And there won't be any problems."

"Okay, Mr. Phost," Dr. Midwiff said. "We're all set. I'll have the emergency kit put together and you can be on your way."

CHAPTER 11

Sitting in the wheelchair with his fat hand resting in the papoose cradle that they had bought, Goodwin's spirits were high as they prepared to leave the hospital.

Kohora pushed the wheelchair down the hall while Goodwin waved at his well wishers. Goodwin had become a curiosity at the hospital.

"It's good to see you in such a lively mood," Kohora said as she playfully ran her hand through her husband's hair. He turned slightly to acknowledge the act.

"It'll be nice to get some home cooking and sleep in my own bed," Goodwin said.

"When this is over and I hope it won't be much longer."

"It shouldn't be," Dr. Midwiff said while he walked with them carrying Goodwin's clothes and Kohora's emergency kit.

When they reached the door, the strapped Goodwin slumped forward in the wheel chair. The straps kept Goodwin from falling from the chair. Kohora grabbed Goodwin's left shoulder. The fat hand rolled up to Goodwin's chest. Dr. Midwiff dropped everything and rushed to help Kohora. He steadied the wheelchair.

"Goodwin! What's wrong? Dr.Midwiff asked, raising Goodwin's head up and pushing his back against the wheelchair. Dr. Midwiff pulled one of Goodwin's eyelids back and was greeted by a blank stare. Blood seeped from the base of the bubble. "Let's turn the chair around and get Goodwin to the emergency. I might have to cut that bubble off."

"Do you think that's necessary?" A worried Kohora asked.

"Yes," Dr. Midwiff replied. "It's getting worse." He took his smock off and wrapped the fat hand in it. When they got to the emergency, "Kohora, will you prep Goodwin for surgery? I'll get a team together."

With the help of two male nurses, Goodwin was placed on the operating table. The fat hand on his left side. Dr. Midwiff was ready.

***

Goodwin was anesthetized. "Scalpel," Dr. Midwiff requested. Kohora placed the sharp instrument in Dr. Midwiff's hand. He made a small incision in the bubble. A steady stream of liquid flowed from the surgical opening. The liquid had a yellowish color, tinged with red. "Get something to catch the fluid."

"What now?" Kohora asked after one of the other surgical team members had brought the container Dr. Midwiff had asked for.

"I'll have to open this up and see what it is," Dr. Midwiff said, shaking his head.

"Brace yourselves. Here goes." Dr. Midwiff finished opening the bubble.

When the bubble had drained its contents, it collapsed around the concealed object that it had protected for the past seven months. Dr. Midwiff reached inside and pulled the life form from its hiding place.

"What the...?" The surgical team exclaimed.

Dr. Midwiff just held it in his hand. "What is this?" Dr. Midwiff asked as he continued to pull at the being, exposing the rest of the abbreviated body. The left hand shuddered.

Dr. Midwiff continued. "Hold this. " He cut the rest of the bubble open, revealing a tapered body with stubby arms and no legs. A kind of Swepea (Popeye's kid) in person.

At the end of the legless individual was a thick cable that trailed down to Goodwin's thumb or what had been his thumb. This was the umbilical cord. "Clamps!" Dr. Midwiff commanded. "I'll have to cut this cord."

When the clamps were put in place, Goodwin passed out, and the unit monitoring Goodwin's vitals went wild. Dr. Midwiff quickly removed the clamps and Goodwin opened his eyes, and the monitoring unit, along with Goodwin's vitals, returned to normal.

"Whew," Dr. Midwiff said with relief as he removed the bubble and its surrounding skin. "Let's clean up this mess," Dr. Midwiff instructed.

"We have to determine what we're going to do until we can separate the two." Kohora spoke. "I'm worried about Goodwin. Will he be all right?" "I don't know," Dr. Midwiff replied, wiping his brow.

The being was cleaned and wrapped in a blanket like any other baby. It was still connected to what was once Goodwin's thumb.

Goodwin stirred. "What's under that blanket?" he asked. Goodwin raised his left hand up as best he could. His eyes followed the cord that led to the blanket. "My hand feels lighter. What's under that blanket? Where's the bubble?" Goodwin wiggled what was left on his thumb. "Did you cut it off?"

"I'm right here," the raspy voice from the baby blanket said. "Did you think you could get rid of me that easily? I'm here to stay . . ."

"Who said that?" The groggy Goodwin asked. He tried to rise up to see where the voice came from.

"Easy, Mr. Phost," Dr. Midwiff said as he placed the blanket tightly over the creature's face in order to muffle any future words. "We've got to get you to your room. Are you hungry? How do you feel?"

Goodwin was silent. "Get me a knife!" Goodwin shouted. "What's under that blanket? Somebody better answer me." Goodwin struggled to sit upright.

***

Goodwin was taken to his old room, where he was strapped to his bed. At first, the little creature was placed on Goodwin's abdomen, but Goodwin went up and down like a bucking bronco and knocked the being against the bed rail. A basket was placed on the side of the bed, and the being was placed in it.

"What shall we call it?" Kohora asked.

Nobody on the team came up with an answer. Finally, Dr. Midwiff spoke, "Let's call it Mese. Short for Siamese. It's almost like a conjoined twin."

"That's fine with me," Mese said. "I wouldn't have liked Goodwin Jr."

Everyone laughed.

"Shut up!" Goodwin shouted. "Let me see what's so funny. Unstrap me and get me a knife and I'll wipe away all those grins."

"And I'll take you with me," Mese said. "I don't like being here anymore than you do.

Don't do me any favors. Give him a knife. I don't care, but I won't go by myself."

"Let me see that piece of crap," Goodwin said. "Let me look at what I've been carrying around for the last six or seven months. I think an abortion is called for."

"Are you sure you want to see Mese?" Dr. Midwiff asked. "It could be traumatic."

"I'm going to have to see it sooner or later. Sooner would be better."

"Let me do it," Kohora said as she bent over and picked Mese up. The basket was rolled to the side, and a stool was placed near the bed for Kohora to sit on while she held Mese. She gradually exposed him to her husband. "Isn't he cute?"

"Ow!" Goodwin said as the umbilical cord that was attached to his thumb was stretched to its limit. "Let me see all of him. I can take it."

Kohora continued to remove the blanket from Mese, revealing his small, grotesque body. Mese was smiling.

"You're kidding," Goodwin said, shaking his head. "This is supposed to be my virus.

Tell me I'm dreaming. Wake me up from this nightmare."

Kohora stopped short of revealing Mese's lower body.

"Where's the rest of him?" Goodwin shouted. "Let me see the whole thing."

Dr. Midwiff pulled the blanket down to Goodwin's thumb while Kohora held Mese as though he were any other baby being shown to its proud parents.

"Do I look like you?" Mese asked. "Which would be okay. I guess?"

Goodwin's negative attitude softened. "I want my life back," he said. "That means we'll have to be separated."

"That could be fatal for both of us. I wouldn't want that to happen," Mese said.

"How long do you think we could exist like this?" Goodwin asked.

"Until you die or when I die; whichever comes first," Mese replied. "Have you wondered why you couldn't leave the hospital?"

Goodwin shook his head. "Did you have anything to do with that?" He asked.

"You bet," Mese said with an impish grin.

"Why?" Goodwin asked.

"For my own survival. I felt safer in the hospital. Do you blame me for being careful?"

"I blame you for everything that has happened to me."

"Like most kids, I didn't ask to be here," Mese said. "Blame yourself. If it wasn't for something you did, I wouldn't be here."

"You won't be here that long," Goodwin said, shaking his head. "I'll see to it."

"What are you saying, dear?" Kohora asked. She continued to hold Mese up so that he faced Goodwin.

Goodwin shook his head. "If any of you think I'm going to be tied to this little bastard forever," he said. "Forget it. I'll find a way to get rid of him."

Mese flashed his most devious grin. "Don't forget," he said. "If you dig a hole for me, dig one for yourself, too." Mese was quiet for a moment.

***

"Have you finished?" An angry Goodwin asked.

Mese ignored Goodwin's question and seemingly went into a trance.

What? No. Goodwin thought. *Not again.* The voice in Goodwin's head was back.

You're never going home. Or should I say we're never going to leave the hospital? I feel very secure here. Who knows what you might do to me if we left the hospital?

"Dear, are you alright?" Kohora asked. "Why are you covering your ears. Do you have an earache? Let me check them for you."

"I'm okay," Goodwin said. "There was a quick ringing in my ears, but it went away."

"Are you sure?" She asked. "You look . . . I don't quite know how to describe it. Are you sure. Don't be so macho. We'd understand after what you've been through."

"There's nothing to understand," Goodwin said, trying to sound as convincing as he could. *If I tell them about the voice,* he thought. *They'll think I've lost it.*

"They sure will." The voice in Goodwin's mind said.

"I'm not done with you!" Goodwin shouted.

"You're not done with who?" Kohora and Dr. Midwiff asked at the same time. Goodwin was silent.

Mese smiled and wiggled his condensed body. He almost slipped from Kohora's grip.

"I was talking to that dummy," Goodwin said, pointing at Mese.

"What has Mese done for you to feel the way you do?" Kohora asked. "It's not his fault that the two of you are bound together."

"Why are you taking his side?" Goodwin asked. "I want him to cut away from me. At this point, I don't care how."

"Even if your life is in danger?" Dr. Midwiff asked. "That's what would happen. Well Mr. Phost, what will it be? We'll work something out. Do you still want to go home?"

Mese has made it clear, Goodwin thought. *He's not going to let me go home.*

Goodwin shook his head. "Maybe I'm better off here at the hospital," he replied.

"Why the sudden change of heart?" Dr. Midwiff asked.

Tell them why. The little voice in Goodwin's head said.

"You tell'um," Goodwin said. "With your smart ass."

"Tell us what?" Dr. Midwiff asked.

"Ask the little dummy," Goodwin insisted. "Earlier Mese had said that he didn't want me to go home because he was afraid of what I might do to him."

Kohora shook her head. "I wouldn't let that happen," she said shifting her weight and getting a better hold on Mese. At eleven pounds, he was getting heavy. "I'd better put you in the basket. Goodwin won't be able to hurt you."

"Please don't put me in that basket," Mese said. "I like it better close to you."

Kohora blushed. "You're so sweet to say that," she said pulling Mese close in a light hug. "Are you hungry? Scratch that. It's time for your nap."

"I'm not sleepy," Mese said. "When big boy over there eats, I'll eat."

Goodwin listened and watched. "You little monster. I might not eat."

"You'll eat," Mese said. "I'll see to it."

"Wanna bet?" Goodwin asked. "I don't have to eat. Maybe you do."

"Mr. Phost are you hungry?" Dr. Midwiff asked. "You should have had several meals by now. Have you lost your appetite?"

"No, but I don't have those cravings since that monster was born," Goodwin said flashing his own evil grin. "I hope that's a sign of things to come."

"What's so funny?" Dr. Midwiff asked. "It seems as though since Mese has come to be, you're back to normal."

Goodwin's evil grin remained. "That gives me an idea," he said. "I think I'll fast."

"Relax Mese," Dr. Midwiff interrupted. "When you get home, things will be much better. Goodwin was frustrated, but he'll come around once he gets to know you."

Goodwin shook violently as he tried to free himself from his restraints. "Put that… whatever you call it in the basket," he said. Goodwin glared at Mese. "Get'im outta my sight. Kohora I don't like him being that close to you. I said put him down. Better yet, drop him."

Mese tried to wiggle closer to Kohora. His stubby little arms reached for Kohora's face. He bounced up and down. Kohora had to adjust her grip again.

"Calm yourself," she said. "You almost fell out of my arms." She cradled Mese in her left arm and gently brushed the top of his head. "Don't cry. You'll be okay."

"Are you going to fall for that b.s.?" Goodwin asked. "Can't you see through that phony crap?"

"You know how badly I've wanted a child," Kohora said. "It seems like my desire has been answered for the time being."

"A very short time," Goodwin said. "He's not a baby. I don't know what he is."

"He's a human like us," Kohora declared. "Please don't forget it." She continued to stroke the little bundle. "I hope we'll be able to take him home…"

"I don't want to go home," Goodwin said. "I'd spend the rest of my life here if it Meant…on second thought, let's go home."

"No!" Mese shouted. "You can't go home. I won't let you."

"Mese, I'm ashamed of you," Kohora said. "I want my husband home. I assure you I won't let him hurt you."

Mese looked at Kohora with tearful eyes. "What's going to happen when you go to work? He could do whatever he wanted."

"You won't have to worry about that," Kohora said, smiling. "Dr. Midwiff said he would assign me to care for my husband. So there's no need for you to worry."

Mese was quiet again as if he were in deep thought.

You're back. Goodwin thought as he reacted to the little voice in his head.

"Remember what happened the last time you tried to leave," the voice in Goodwin's mind said. *"If you try, I'll have to punish you again."*

Goodwin shot back at Mese with his own telepathic message. *We'll see. You little monster. I'll tell Kohora what you're planning. You can't prove it. I'll deny everything.* Mese thought back at Goodwin.

"When can we leave?" The angry Goodwin asked as loudly as he could. The bed shook while Goodwin tried to free himself.

"Are you sure?" Dr. Midwiff asked, considering what has happened in the past."

Goodwin nodded.

"We'll try one more time, but if anything goes wrong, you'll have to stay at the hospital until we can amputate."

"Why don't you go ahead and amputate now?" Goodwin asked.

"We don't want to endanger your life if we can get around it," Dr. Midwiff answered.

"Will the little monster be in any danger?"

"Of course," Dr. Midwiff replied.

"Then do it," Goodwin said with a big smile.

"It's not that simple," Dr. Midwiff said. "We can't knowingly endanger either of your lives. We're looking into as many possibilities as might be safe. Since you and Mese don't share a major organ, there really shouldn't be a big problem separating you two."

"There is one minor problem," Dr. Midwiff said. "Mese gets his nourishment from you by way of that cord that tapers down to your thumb. Mese doesn't have a stomach."

"So that's why I was always hungry?" Goodwin interrupted. "The little parasite."

Dr. Midwiff paused and rubbed his chin. "Mese could probably survive on an IV diet."

He said, "But for how long, I don't know."

"I should have a say in this," Mese said. "It's my life too."

"That might be true," Dr. Midwiff said, "but you're in a...How should I say it? Mr. Phost has a say in it too, and he's not too pleased with you."

"I'm glad to hear that somebody is concerned about me," Goodwin said. "I don't have anything against that little parasite, but the sooner we're cut away from each other, it'll be better for both of us. I'll still hurt him if I get the chance."

Mese frowned. "That goes double for me," he said. "If you try to leave the hospital, I'll make your life a living hell. Remember what happened just before I was . . ."

"Hatched!" Goodwin shouted. "H-a-t-c-h-e-d." Goodwin broke into a loud guffaw.

Mese dropped his head and reached for Kohora. "I'm human like all of you. Chickens are hatched," he said. "I didn't choose to be here. I hope I'll be allowed to be somebody."

"You are already somebody," Kohora assured Mese. "Once the problem of separating you from my husband is solved, you'll see. Both of you will have to be civil toward each other. Is that understood?"

"No," Goodwin said. "Never. I'm ready to go home."

Mese raised his head in a goose-necked formation. "I don't want to go," he said.

"I'm scared."

"Are we going?" Goodwin asked.

"If you insist," an angry Mese said. "I'll have to take over and help myself. I'm not going to tell you again. You can't leave the hospital unless I say so."

"I'll take my chances," Goodwin said. "If I can't leave, they had better be prepared for an all-out disruption. I'll break that cord one way or another."

Kohora and Dr. Midwiff looked at each other. Both of them shook their heads.

"What's wrong?" Goodwin asked. "There's no reason to keep me here."

Finally, Dr. Midwiff spoke. "Mr. Phost, I do believe you'd be better off at home. Sorry Mese, but Goodwin has the last word. Kohora will keep a close eye on Goodwin."

Goodwin smiled, and Mese smiled underneath his croc tears.

Everything was packed as before. Mese was placed in the papoose pouch, which was strapped to Goodwin's chest, which allowed the two beings to face each other. Goodwin's left hand was bound to the wheelchair's armrest, and his right hand was also bound to the other armrest. Dr. Midwiff carried the necessary bags, and Kohora pushed Goodwin in the wheelchair. As they neared the exit, Kohora paused. Globules of sweat oozed from Goodwin's forehead.

Why am I sweating so? Goodwin asked himself. *I know. I'm afraid of what might happen when we get to the door.*

"What's wrong, dear?" Kohora asked Goodwin. "Don't you want to leave 'this place' as you put it." Mese sneered. Dr. Midwiff went ahead to open the door.

"Wait!" Goodwin shouted. "I'm worried. Am I going to be able to leave?" Goodwin closed his eyes. "If I pass out, keep going. If those attacks come, I'll scream and bear it."

Kohora slowed her pace, and Dr. Midwiff took a deep breath and slowly opened the door. Goodwin struggled with the straps that bound his arms to the wheelchair. The door swung open, and Kohora quickly pushed Goodwin through the door. Everybody let out a big sigh of relief.

***

"I feel so free," Goodwin exclaimed when the outside air swept across his face.

"I don't know how you did it," The voice in Goodwin's head declared. *"But it's not over. I'll gain control again, and next time it could be fatal. You hear me? Fatal!"*

"You've lost your power to keep me at the hospital," Goodwin shot back via their telepathic connection. His lips moved with every word. *"I didn't do anything. I wish I could like stop you from breathing."*

"Who are you talking to?" Kohora asked.

"Nobody," Goodwin lied. "Thinking out loud…I guess. Let's get to the car."

At the car, "Goodwin, we'll have to release your hands," Dr. Midwiff said. "Kohora do you think it's safe to do so?"

Kohora looked at Goodwin. "Do I have your word that you'll behave yourself and not try to hurt Mese?" She asked. "I mean it, Goodwin. Don't blow this. If you do . . ."

"You'll be put in a straitjacket," Dr. Midwiff interrupted. "And treated like any other nut case until this problem is solved.

"Not only that," Kohora interjected, "but I wouldn't be able to live with you."

"You wouldn't be able to live with me," Goodwin repeated. "And what for?"

"Don't forget that Mese is human, too," Kohora said. "Give him some respect."

"What choice do I have?" Goodwin asked.

"You know the rules," Mese sent Goodwin another telepathic message.

Goodwin spoke directly to Mese. "What's so funny?" He asked.

"The insults will have to stop," Kohora insisted. "Mese has feelings too."

"Okay, okay," Goodwin said in a disgruntled tone. "I got the message."

Kohora rolled Goodwin around to the front passenger side. She slowly removed the straps from Goodwin's arms. "And don't forget your promises," she said.

I could smash this little monster, but that would be exactly what he wants. Goodwin thought. *He could stop me from leaving the hospital again.*

"Why the grim look?" Goodwin asked, staring right at Mese.

Mese didn't answer, but he sent Goodwin another telepathic message. *"You win again. Enjoy while you can".*

Kohora interrupted the mental jousting. She opened the door. "Goodwin, get in the car," she said. "I thought you were in a hurry to get to the house."

"Yeah. Get into the car," Mese repeated. "I want to see my new home."

Goodwin slid in and awkwardly placed the papoose pouch with Mese in it on his chest. There was a slot at the bottom of the pouch that allowed Mese's tapered body to fit.

With Kohora's help, Goodwin managed to put the seatbelt on. It was placed between him and Mese's pouch. Dr. Midwiff placed the cart for Mese in the trunk and returned to the hospital. Kohora drove.

CHAPTER 12

At their house, Kohora helped Goodwin out of the car. He went inside to the living room and sat in his big easy chair. Then she unpacked everything. Mese had fallen asleep.

"Is there anything I can get you?" Kohora asked. "A soda, a snack?"

Without answering, Goodwin reflected on his situation. *I shoulda stayed at the hospital with this parasite. How am I going to function with this thing hanging onto me?*

Eating, sleeping, crapping, making love to my wife. This isn't going to work.

"I'm waiting," Kohora said. "Is there anything I can get for you?"

I would like to say a knife. Goodwin reflected. "I'm sorry," Goodwin replied. "What did you say? My mind was elsewhere. This . . ."

"Don't you dare," Kohora said. "Mese might hear you. Remember your promise?"

She went to the kitchen to prepare dinner.

Mese opened his eyes and winked at Goodwin. *"You had better watch yourself,"* Mese said in his telepathic message to Goodwin.

Thump! Went the middle finger of Goodwin's right hand upside Mese's forehead.

"Ow!" Mese cried. "Don't do that. If Kohora found out, you'd be in trouble."

"Who's going to tell her?" Goodwin asked while covering Mese's mouth with his hand. "If you get too smart, I might have to take you out promise or no promise. And don't you forget it." Goodwin removed his hand from Mese's mouth.

Gasping for air, Mese said, "I…I don't believe you."

"Try me!" Goodwin said. "My word against yours. You can't prove it."

"We've got to go back to the hospital," Mese said in a telepathic message to Goodwin.

"I like it better here," Goodwin said. Returning the message.

"Goodwin," Kohora said from the kitchen. "Is Mese okay?"

"I'm not his babysitter," Goodwin answered. "Ask him."

"I asked you," Kohora said. "Is he okay?"

Mese opened his eyes and grinned at Goodwin.

"Don't forget what I told you," Goodwin said. "And I'm making sure you hear me."

"Dinner is almost ready," Kohora said. "I hope you'll like it."

"What are you so happy about?" Goodwin asked Mese. "You can't eat. You don't have any teeth."

"I can still enjoy a tasty meal," Mese said, even if I can't taste it."

"Come and get it!" Kohora shouted.

"Oh goody," Mese said with gleeful anticipation.

Goodwin got up from his easy chair and went to the small dining room.

***

Goodwin grabbed Mese by his little nightshirt and removed him from the papoose pouch and placed him in the basket they had brought from the hospital.

"Careful with Mese," Kohora warned. "Let me help you."

"I've finished," Goodwin said. He gave Mese his meanest stare. "You lie there and don't say a word. Let me enjoy my dinner."

Lying on his back, Mese looked up at the ceiling. "Eat enough for both of us," he said.

"I wish I didn't have to eat at all," Goodwin said. "Maybe I could get rid of you."

"Be nice," Kohora said, pointing her finger at Goodwin. "You'll get used to him."

"Never," Goodwin said between bites. "I'll be glad when Midwiff and Wells decide what are they going to do with it?"

"I'm not an it!" Mese said, and I don't like being called such."

"You yelling at me?" Goodwin asked. "I'll show you…"

"No, you won't," Kohora said, grabbing Goodwin's right hand before he backhanded Mese. "You want to go back to the hospital don't you?"

Goodwin smiled. "It must be your mother instinct," he said as he allowed Kohora to stop the descent of his hand against Mese's baby face. "I wasn't going to hit him. Just scare him a little."

Mese had twisted his little body to the side, trying to avoid the blow. "I'm scared,"

He said. "Maybe the hospital is the best place for me. A twenty-four-hour guard, too."

"Goodwin didn't mean it," Kohora said. "He feels so confined. Mese would you accept an apology?"

"I'll think about it," Mese replied with a big grin.

"You had better say yes," Goodwin shot Mese a telepathic message.

"And if I don't," Mese came right back via the mental airways.

"If you don't," Goodwin said.

"And if he doesn't?" Kohora asked.

"Oops," Goodwin said. "Just thinking out loud…" He paused.

"And if I don't?" Mese shot another telepathic message, followed by another smirk.

"You win for now, but watch your tail," Goodwin replied through the mental airways.

"I don't have a tail," Mese said. "My legs just didn't develop."

"Goodwin!" Kohora shouted. "What did you say to Mese?"

"I was kidding," Goodwin said. "Mese took it the wrong way."

"I won't tolerate you insulting Mese," Kohora said. "Maybe you want to go back to the hospital. I mean it! Treat Mese with respect." Mese watched in silence as Goodwin's expression changed.

Goodwin reached over and picked Mese up from the tray.

"What are you doing?" The frightened Mese asked. "Put me down."

"I've got to pee," Goodwin said, putting Mese back in the papoose pouch. "If it's okay with you. Let's go."

***

In the bathroom, Goodwin remained standing while he opened his pants and peed. He flushed the toilet and zipped his pants up. *"I'd like to flush you away too,"* Goodwin's telepathic message to Mese said, *"But maybe later."*

"Go ahead and do it," Mese shot back via the telepathic airways. *"I've had it. I don't want to live like this. You could say I jumped out of this pouch and did it myself."*

Goodwin ignored Mese's request and washed his hands the best he could. They returned to the kitchen, where Goodwin placed Mese back in the tray and finished his meal. Goodwin rolled the tray into the living room, where he sat down in his easy chair and tried to relax.

***

Goodwin's thoughts were interrupted by a message from Mese.

"Why didn't you drown me in the commode after you peed?" Mese asked through the telepathic airways. *"If you really want to relax, you'd better answer me."*

"Go to sleep," Goodwin said, shaking his fist at Mese. *"I'll get my chance, and you won't know what hit you."*

"And where will you live after that?" Mese asked via the mind waves. *"You love your wife don't you? What did she tell you would happen if you did anything to me?"* Mese winked at Goodwin and smiled.

"Ow!" Mese yelled as Goodwin yanked on the cord that connected the two beings.

"What's going on in there?" Kohora inquired from the kitchen. "Goodwin, what are you doing to Mese?"

"Nothing!" Goodwin shouted. "He must have had some kind of pain. You know . . . us being tied together and all." Goodwin gestured for Mese not to answer. He reached over and placed his hand over Mese's mouth.

Mese struggled to remove Goodwin's hand from his mouth, and his baby-like hands were powerless against Goodwin's powerful hand.

When Mese didn't answer, Kohora rushed to the living room where Goodwin's hand still covered Mese's face.

"What are you doing to Mese?" She asked. "That's it. You'll have to go back to the hospital. You were warned. I can't watch you all the time."

"Ha, ha." Mese laughed in Goodwin's mind. *"I'll be safe again."*

"I'm sorry," Goodwin answered via the mind while removing his hand from Mese's face. *"Will you forgive me?"*

"That won't get it," Mese said aloud. "Let Kohora hear it, too."

"Let me hear what?" Kohora asked, looking directly at Goodwin.

"I don't know what came over me," Goodwin said. "I'm really sorry."

"Tell Mese," Kohora said. "Look at him."

"Why do you always take his side?" Goodwin asked.

"I don't take sides," Kohora said. "I call it like I see it. Why did you have your hand over Mese's face?"

"I…I was trying to relax and he wouldn't shut up," Goodwin replied. "Before I knew it, my hand was over his mouth."

"I didn't hear Mese talking," Kohora said.

"Trust me," Goodwin said. "You see…we can converse through our minds. We're still connected and Mese sent me those mental messages."

"You mean there's a mental connection between the two of you?" The astonished Kohora asked. "You can read each other's minds?"

"Something like that," Goodwin answered.

"How long has this been going on?" Kohora asked. "Who else knows about this?"

"Just you," Goodwin answered. "It was no big deal. I had heard voices long before Mese arrived, but I thought it was all in my head."

***

Kohora looked at Mese, then at her husband. "Are you sure?" She asked." Can you prove it? *That's why Goodwin was talking to himself.* She recalled.

"And that's not all," Goodwin said, interrupting Kohora's muse. "The little brat also kept me from leaving the hospital."

"How?" Kohora asked. "He wasn't here."

"I don't know how he did it, but before he was…"

"Born!" Kohora said. "How could he? We left the hospital. Explain that."

"Ask him," Goodwin said.

"I don't know, and if I did, I wouldn't tell." Mese sent another psychic message.

"Mese, why were we able to leave the hospital?" Kohora asked.

Mese had turned his head and closed his eyes. *"Are you trying to make me look bad?"* He asked Goodwin through his psychic projection.

"Mese, I'm waiting," Kohora said. "Why were we able to leave the hospital?"

"No. I'm not trying to make you look bad," Goodwin answered aloud.

"Who're you talking to?" Kohora asked. "Has your mental state regressed? And don't tell me you're talking to Mese because he's asleep."

"He's not asleep," Goodwin said, reaching over and shaking Mese. "Wake up!"

Mese remained silent. *"We'll be back in the hospital before you know it,"* Mese said via his telepathic medium.

"Let him alone," Kohora said.

"You don't believe me do you?" The angry and frustrated Goodwin asked.

"Ha, ha, ha," Mese laughed, sending Goodwin a mental chuckle.

Goodwin reached over and grabbed Mese by his little nightshirt and held him up.

"You dummy. . . I won't do this," Goodwin said, and he dropped Mese back in the tray.

"If you think we're going back to the hospital, think again."

"I'm not a dummy," Mese explained. "I can think for myself, but… what if I were a dummy? That is working with a ventriloquist. I could make money and help pay some of those bills."

"You're connected to me," Goodwin said, raising his left hand up, exposing the cord that connected them." What are you going to do about that?"

"Disconnect me," Mese answered, smiling. "You'd like that wouldn't you?"

"You are slick," Goodwin said. "You want to get me back to that hospital. Not a chance. I almost fell into your little trap."

"Mese, Goodwin. Stop it!" Kohora said. "Let's calm down and talk this through."

"There's nothing to talk about," Mese said, sporting a big grin that engulfed his tiny face. He clapped his hands. "I can hardly wait to get back to that good ole hospital."

I don't like Mese's tone. Kohora thought. *It sounds a little arrogant.* "We will talk about it," she said. "I'd rather have the two of you here."

"You saw what happened the minute Goodwin was out of your sight," Mese said. "He tried to smother me. If we were separated, you wouldn't have to worry about me."

"He might have had a good reason to," Kohora said. "You're beginning to sound conceited. I'm aware of your condition, but Goodwin is still my husband, and I won't turn against him for anybody."

In a restrained tone, "I understand," Mese said, but he has been mean to me. Let the doctors disconnect us, and we can go our separate ways."

"Sounds like a good idea," Kohora said, "but where would you go?"

"If I could find a sponsor," Mese said. "I could pull the bucks in."

"Doing what?" Kohora asked.

"I could be somebody's dummy," Mese replied. "Like in ventriloquism."

"Goodwin. What do you think?" Kohora asked. "Maybe we could sponsor Mese.

Until then, there must be mutual respect between both of you," Kohora said.

Mese held his undersized arms up and thrust them in Goodwin's direction. "Can we be friends?" He asked.

Goodwin looked at Kohora. She nodded her approval.

***

What is Mr. Slick up to now? Goodwin asked himself. *I don't trust him.*

"Goodwin!" Kohora said. "Will you be Mese's friend?"

"Friend is kinda strong," Goodwin replied, but I'll try to be more civilized if he'll let me. It'll be bedtime in a few hours." *I don't know how this is going to work.* Goodwin thought. *He's definitely going to sleep in his tray.*

"That's all I could ask for," Kohora said, taking one of Mese's diminutive hands in her right hand. "Goodwin, give me your hand. We're now one big happy circle of friends."

After the ceremonial truce, Mese spoke. "Like I said, we'd make one hell of a team. I'd be the dummy, and Goodwin could be the ventriloquist. What do you think?"

Goodwin pondered over the question. "How would we go about doing something like that?" Goodwin asked. "You're a real person."

"Thank you," Mese said. "Thank you. Thank you. I am a person."

"You didn't answer my Question," Goodwin said. "There are a lot of things to be done. Do you have a game plan?"

"Oh! Yes, I do," Mese replied. "First, I'd have to have a wooden-looking face to hide my human appearance." Mese winked at Goodwin. "Think about it. You'd be able to do what no other ventriloquist has ever done."

"Like what?" Goodwin asked.

"Think about it," Mese said. "For starters, you might not have to move your lips or pause and turn sideways to conceal what you might be doing. You could we could sing together. You could make sure that your lips were occupied while you continued to make me talk. Not to mention the money we could bring in."

Goodwin listened. He had always wanted to be in show business.

"It's bedtime," Goodwin said. "We can talk about this tomorrow. Okay?"

"Okay," Mese answered. "I thought it was quite an idea." He closed his eyes and pretended to be asleep.

Kohora went over and made sure that Mese was tucked in. She paused and pulled the baby blanket that the hospital had provided a little farther up on Mese.

Mese continued his charade.

"What are you doing?" Goodwin asked. "Let's go to bed."

"Shh," Kohora whispered. "Don't wake Mese up."

"He's going to have to wake up," Goodwin said.

"Why?"

"I have to put my PJs on," Goodwin answered. "Do you think he'll sleep through it?"

"If we're quiet," Kohora answered. "I'll help you."

***

"Here we go," Goodwin said, standing up from his side of the bed. Kohora helped his shorts off and put his PJ bottom on. He slept topless because of his connection to Mese. Goodwin eased back onto the bed. His left arm, which was connected to Mese, hung over the side where Mese rested in his tray.

"You could let Mese sleep on your chest," she said.

"Are you kidding? One connection is enough for me," Goodwin said. "I can't stand that little . . . person."

Kohora got in on the other side of the bed and snuggled close to Goodwin. Mese stirred, but didn't wake up. Kohora reached over and grabbed Goodwin's private. It was standing at attention. She stroked it several times.

"Wow," Goodwin said in an exaggerated whisper. "Can we go a little further?"

"You read my mind," Kohora said. "You're not allergic to me anymore are you?"

Kohora carefully mounted Goodwin. She gently moved up and down.

"Uuuhuu," Goodwin moaned. "I'm almost there. Uuuhu."

"Don't you cry out," Kohora cautioned. "We don't want to wake Mese up."

After they finished, Kohora washed up, then she washed Goodwin off. After taking the pan and towels she had used to clean Goodwin, Kohora returned to the bed. Goodwin rolled over on his right side, and Kohora backed into him, and both of them fell asleep.

CHAPTER 13

Mese lay awake with his eyes closed. Illusions of grandeur filled his little mind. He nodded in and out of wakefulness. His fantasies took over. *Free at last.* He thought. *This is what I've wanted for as long as I can remember.* Mese looked around. He rubbed his Lilliputian body all over. *No more Goodwin. I can walk. No tapered body. The operation was successful. No umbilical cord.*

Mese walked over to the bed where Goodwin was asleep. "Wake up," Mese said. "It's time for our show."

Goodwin stirred. "What?" He asked. "I must have slept longer than I thought."

"You did," Mese said. "I'll go over to the dresser and put my dummy mask on."Mese went over to the dresser and climbed onto the chair. He tried to slip the dummy over his head, but the mask didn't cooperate. "Can you help me with this mask?"

"In a minute," Goodwin answered.

Mese put his performing jacket on. The jacket had a side pocket in the back where Goodwin slipped his left hand, which made it appear that he was controlling Mese's movements. *I hope we can cut tonight's show a little short.* Mese thought. This *mask gets hot...* "Goodwin, are you up?" Mese asked his performing buddy. "We'll go on in a minute."

"Keep your shirt on," Goodwin said. "We have a few minutes before showtime."

"Just checking," Mese said. "I still need your help with this mask."

"Give me a minute," Goodwin answered.

"I'll wait here," Mese said, admiring himself in the mirror.

They were doing nightly shows at the Wiltern Theater in Los Angeles, where they were the main attraction.

"That should do it," Goodwin said while he made the final adjustment to the mask."

"We're all set. Let's go and knock 'em dead."

They left their room and followed the hallway that led to the stage. Mese and Goodwin took their places just before the curtains opened. Goodwin sat in a chair with Mese on his lap. "Smile," Goodwin said. "At least do the dummy smile."

***

"Ladies and gentlemen," the master of ceremonies said. "It's my pleasure to present to you the world's foremost ventriloquist, **Goodwin The Greaaat!** I know what you're thinking. You might think you've seen the best, but before you leave tonight, you'll know that you have not come close to seeing the best."

In hushed tones, Mese and Goodwin talked to each other. "I wish he'd hurry so we can do the show and get out of here," Mese said. "This wooden dummy mask is hot."

"Patience, ole buddy," Goodwin whispered back." We don't want our audience to Know that you're not a dummy, but a living, breathing human."

"So!" Mese said. "You concede that I am human. What do you think they'd do if they knew I was human?"

"They would run us off stage and out of town," Goodwin replied. "They paid big bucks to see us.

"This is our seventh straight night and I'm tired," Mese said in an undertone. "I didn't sleep good last night. I haven't slept worth a damn all this week.

"What's your problem?" Goodwin asked. "I sleep sound every night."

"If I was getting what you get every night, I'd sleep sound, too," Mese said.

"What's that supposed to mean?" Goodwin asked.

"A beautiful woman like Kohora to rock me every night, I'd sleep sound, too," Mese replied. "You're one lucky sucker."

"Without any further delay," the MC said, "Here's the one, the only, Goodwin with his pal Mese. Let's giv'em a big hand."

Meek clapping of hands followed the MC's introduction.

"Come on. You can do better," the MC spoke louder. **"Let's hear it for Goodwin and his sidekick, Mese the Magnificent. Enjoy the show."**

The crowd responded.

"Are you nervous?" Goodwin whispered to Mese.

"No. I'm not," Mese answered. "I want to do the show and get out of here."

All eyes were on Mese. That made it seem all the more real. There was a tiny wireless mike, that was patched into the theater's sound system.

Goodwin stared out at the audience. Then at Mese. Goodwin had mastered the art of slightly moving his lips and making his throat muscles pulsate in sync with Mese's lips. Mese took the mike in his mini-hand and began to speak.

"Let's hear it for Goodwin," he said. "Not only is he the foremost ventriloquist of the modern era, but for all times. Don't be bashful, Goodwin. Say something."

Mese moved his lips slightly and bowed his head up and down. Taking the regular mike from its stand, Goodwin said, "That's what I get for letting this dummy has too much freedom."

Mese continued to mock Goodwin's role as the performer. His lips moved ever so slightly to the rhythm of Goodwin's facial expressions. The crowd went crazy.

One guy in the audience stood up. "Now we know who the real dummy is," he said.

The crowd went positively nuts.

"I resent that," Goodwin said.

"Okay," Goodwin said. "It's my turn."

Mese followed the cue. Goodwin worked his lips ever so slightly.

"I'm sorry," Mese said, dropping his head.

"Don't look at me," Goodwin said, pretending to be angry. "Look at our illustrious fans. They deserve to be treated better. Shall we get on with the show?" Goodwin picked up a glass of water that was close by. He began to drink, making loud noises to make sure there wasn't any doubt that he was actually drinking the water.

Mese coughed. "Excuse me," he said, "but something went down the ole airway."

Goodwin continued to drink the water, making sure he threw in a couple of sloppy slurps. The show continued as Goodwin continued to eat and drink while supposedly making Mese talk. When the performance ended, they were rushed to their suite. Fans were everywhere. Security was tight.

***

Once they were safely behind closed doors, Mese and Goodwin began to argue.

"We're going to stop doing shows every night," Mese said. "It's too much for me."

"The money is good," Goodwin said, removing the fake dummy face that Mese wore during the performance. "Besides, you don't have to do anything but relax and sleep.

"When we get enough money," Mese said. "Maybe I could have my own cute little chick and get laid every night . . ."

"Stop dreaming," Goodwin said. "You know that's not going to happen."

"I can wish. Can't I?" Mese asked with tears streaming down his face.

"Stop it!" Goodwin shouted. "You're free from me. Let that do for now. Your life is already better."

"The only thing that could make my life better would be to be born again," Mese said.

"Make that a normal birth with two parents who would love me."

"I really feel for you," Goodwin said. "I'd give anything to make sure it had never happened."

"If you feel that way," Mese said. "Why don't you kill me and put me out of this miserable existence? If I were able, I'd do it myself."

"We'll go home tonight," Goodwin said. "Maybe Kohora can cheer you up."

***

Back at the house, Mese stirred. Then he cried out. "Somebody, help me! I can't live like this anymore."

The outburst startled Goodwin and Kohora. She hopped out of bed and ran to the other side where the frightened Mese lay in his tray.

"Mese, what's wrong?" She asked, scooping Mese up from the tray. "Were you having a nightmare? Are you in pain?" Kohora cradled Mese in her arms and rocked him back and forth. "Please stop crying. Whatever it was, you're safe now."

You have a way about you. Mese thought as the scent of her warm breasts brought some relief to his grief. Between sobs, "I was awake all night," Mese said. "Fantasizing that Goodwin and I had been separated, but when it ended, that's when I cried out. Reality is a B."

Goodwin had listened to the conversation. Finally, he spoke, "Kohora, put him down. He wants sympathy plain and simple."

"Let me enjoy the moment!" Mese shouted. He tried to cuddle even closer to Kohora.

"If this is what I have to look forward to," Goodwin said, "let's take him back to the hospital and cut him loose."

"No! No!" Mese screamed. "I don't want to be separated from Goodwin. What would I do? Where would I go? I'd miss you, too."

"I'll bet that's the main reason you don't want to be cut loose. We can't spend the rest of our lives connected," Goodwin said. "Sooner or later, we'll have to part sooner the better." Goodwin caught himself, but it was too late. Tears flowed freely from Mese.

"Goodwin. You should be ashamed," Kohora said. "We're all that Mese has. There must be something we can do if and when he's separated from you."

"Nobody cares about me," Mese said between sobs. "I wish I were dead."

"You don't mean that," Kohora said. She continued to console Mese. The sobs finally ceased. Mese had drifted off to sleep. Kohora bent over and gently placed Mese back in the tray, pulling the baby blanket up to his chin. "I think I'll spend the rest of the night on the couch. I warned you about saying unkind words to Mese."

"If you do," Goodwin said. "I won't be responsible for what happens to that brat."

"You want to go back to the hospital. Don't you?" Kohora asked. "That's where you're going if anything happens to Mese."

She really pisses me off when she talks like that. Goodwin pondered. "I'm not going back to the hospital," he said. "If you don't come back to bed, nobody's going to get any sleep tonight. **Especially Mese!"**

"We are going back to the hospital first thing in the morning."

Their bickering woke Mese up. "Keep it down," he said. "I'm trying to sleep."

"Shut your trap," Goodwin said, jerking on the umbilical cord that the two men shared.

"If you were asleep, you wouldn't have heard us."

"Ow!" Mese screamed. "Kohora, help me."

"Goodwin. What are you doing?" Kohora asked. "I see you are determined to hurt Mese. It's not good for our relationship. I'm still not going to sleep with you tonight."

Goodwin gave the cord two more powerful jerks while he laughed at Mese's agony.

"Owee! Owee!" Mese screamed.

Goodwin continued to jerk the cord. Blood had begun to seep from the cord.

Hearing the screams, Kohora rushed over and placed her arm around Goodwin's right shoulder. "Easy, dear," Kohora said. "Calm down."

"I won't calm down!" Goodwin said.

"There! That should hold you, "Kohora said as she jabbed the hypodermic needle with the fast-acting sedative into the side of Goodwin's neck.

"What did you do to me?" Goodwin asked. His jerking on the umbilical cord turned to a twitch.

When Goodwin woke up the next morning, he was back in the hospital. Dr. Midwiff, Dr. Wells and Kohora were at his bedside.

"What happened to Mese? My hand?" Goodwin asked, holding his bandaged hand in the air. I hope it's what I think it is. We're separated forever. Where's the little bugger?"

Silence was the only response Goodwin received.

"Did I say something wrong?" Goodwin asked. "Why the long faces?" He waved his bandaged hand in a jubilant gesture. "Say something. The operation was a success."

"Yes," Kohora said, holding back her tears. "But we lost Mese!"

"What?" Goodwin asked. "Say that again."

"We lost Mese," the two doctors and Kohora replied in unison.

"I hope you're satisfied," Kohora said. "I need some time alone."

"Don't leave like this," Goodwin pleaded. "I still love and need you."

"Do you know what Mese's last words were?" She asked.

Goodwin shook his head.

"'Tell Goodwin I still like him, and I hoped that we could have pulled off that ventriloquist act that I had fantasized about. I know that in another time and place, we would have knocked'em dead.' Kohora continued, "I had some good news for you too, but I don't feel like talking about it."

"Take this and wipe your eyes," Dr. Midwiff said, handing Kohora a tissue.

"What's the good news?" Goodwin asked. "Don't keep me in the dark. Please don't."

"Should I tell him?" Kohora asked the two doctors. "He's so happy that Mese is out of his life, I wonder if any other news could make him happy . . ."

"Try me!" Goodwin shouted.

"I'm pregnant!"